GLADSTONE

A Novel

GLADSTONE

A Novel

Ken A Locke

Chimenea Press
chimeneapress.com

979-8-9991709-0-3 (paperback)
979-8-9991709-1-0 (ebook)

To Mom and Dad, who have listened to me
make up stories for a very long time.

Contents

Author's Note

There is a place in New Mexico called Gladstone. It is a small wideout on US Route 56 in between Clayton and Springer. Wikipedia has this to say: "Gladstone is an unincorporated layover in Union County, New Mexico, United States, founded in 1880. It lies at the intersection of US Route 56 and Union County Road C001. The post office, which opened in 1888, closed in 2010, leaving only a general store with gas service, and two houses, located there."

When I drove past there on a trip with my dad, we stopped to see what it was all about. This story came to me in a few phrases then, and soon became this novel you are about to read.

This novel is entirely fiction, and any resemblance or coincidence to real life that exists on the eastern plains of New Mexico is entirely by chance. I don't know if the store is still open, but I know the land exists and holds me in its thrall to this day.

Well. I won't live forever. And someone needs to take over who can keep Gladstone a haven. I'm not sure if any of those three can do that. Not sure at all.

Hazel Gladstone

Chapter 1

Hazel

If I had known that I'd live the rest of my life out here in the middle of the desert, wishing for a tornado to come and liven things up, I would never have taken that last ride back from Springer, where I quit going to school in the sixth grade. I'd a just stayed there and worked in the Brown Hotel kitchen. I know that I'm the glue that holds Gladstone Property together—they are all so demanding!—but, my word, it gets exhausting.

It was a little better before Travis went senile. He could at least carry on a conversation at the supper table. Nowadays, he just smiles and eats without most of the manners he learned as a boy.

Shelly has plenty of manners, but glory, she is morose. Ever since she showed up, however many years ago, and walked straight back to the arroyo, she's been a puzzle. Of course we let her stay, and of course she's been a blessing, but who just shows up and then stays the rest of her life? She didn't even ever want to go back home and see if her folks were ok. I've walked with her past the old sod, and out to the spring, but she hears nothing. Not the good nor the bad. That's fine, but it falls to me to explain.

Thank God Claire finally showed up! I can at least feel like the place will be in good hands once I pass on. That's coming soon, I'm pretty sure. My dreams are always pretty clear about that: "Find a replacement; then job done." I'm not sure how Claire convinced her mama to run out here, Claire being a baby and all, but it's a darned good thing she did, even if Opal is a complete and hopeless mess. I'm willing to bet that Opal was a far bigger problem to her baby daddy than he was to her. But you won't catch me saying that out loud.

Back when I was eight, back when Mother and Father were alive, and Uncle Nathan was alive and not yet turned, I felt like Gladstone was the perfect place for all of us to live. We could just park the truck a week at a time, plant our little garden, tend our cows and pigs. I'd watch Daddy, Travis, and Nathan build Gladstone House, counting the days before we could move out of that spider-hole of a sham adobe house and into the building with a floor that was real wood and not dirt. Mother was so patient. I tried to emulate her example by not complaining. By not crying at bedtime because I was afraid that spiders would sneak down a web and sit next to my ear, and then eventually bite me. Rattlesnakes were a fact of life out here; my job was to avoid them, but then get Daddy to shoot them with the shotgun. Mama wanted to eat them always, but I never did try that meat. It looked bony, in addition to probably carrying the venom with it into the chili.

"No, thank you, I do not care for any," is what I always said.

The voice told me to take in *everyone* who was hurting; that turned out to *be almost everyone* I met on the street. That's why I could barely stand to leave Gladstone. I'd be the Pied Piper—"Come on home, little one… I'll fix you." No matter their age. I could just sense it all, and it broke my heart.

Have I wasted my entire life by caring for just three poor souls? If Claire doesn't stay and take over… Well, we'll see.

Chapter 2

Shelly

"Get out. Stay out. Take your whoring ways somewhere I don't have to be reminded of the frailty of woman."

Her father, a religious zealot from near the rusty buckle of the Bible Belt, wanted nothing to do with her. And that is all he had to say when he found out she was pregnant. Somehow, her boyfriend had convinced her to have sex with her. And, of course, she got pregnant, and it was her problem— her shame—alone. Unfairness heaped upon blame. Shelly had attended junior high, where health class was required, so she knew that babies were possible after one time, but she figured she could beat the odds. Didn't happen. She didn't beat the odds.

That is how Shelly got to this small turnout on the road, Gladstone, way back when she was barely a woman.

That last conversation with her parents still trembled through her spirit, whenever she forgot not to think about home on the edge of the Ozarks. She had gotten on a bus in Joplin and ridden west. She had enough money for a ticket to Las Vegas. The one in New Mexico—not the glittery, cool one farther away. When they stopped in Gladstone for a cold drink, she took a walk along the desert road behind the property. In a funk, she missed the horn of the Trailways bus, which, after five minutes of honking, drove off without her but with her suitcase. It didn't matter, because all she had in her case was old clothes, a pair of scuffed heels, and her mother's Bible.

"Take it, Shelly. You never know when you will turn back to the Lord. If you do, maybe you can write, and I'll see what your father thinks about taking you back in," her mother had said about the Bible. Well-meaning, clueless, sheltered—her mother, defined.

Clueless that Shelly was filled with a fury that would always prevent her from a happy homecoming. Hell, it would prevent her from *any* homecoming. It didn't make sense to tell any of that to her mother as they clung to each other for those last few seconds. Shelly just murmured into her hair, crooning words of comfort and love that rang with a fake hope. Her father had just stared at her, lifted one hand to waist height when she turned to face him. Didn't step forward to hug her, didn't smile, didn't hand her any money.

"I hope you're happy, Dad."

Shelly turned from her parents, walked up the block and around the corner, and out of their lives. Though she didn't know it, she would never see them alive again.

Shelly, when she was young and new to Gladstone, had sun-tipped blonde hair that ran down to her shoulder blades in liquid waves. Not curly, but not barn-board straight, either. She paid little attention to it. She enjoyed washing it in the spring water the old-fashioned way, even though there was a hot water heater and a gravity plumbing system that worked perfectly well in the house. Her first few years at Gladstone, she'd gotten used to cold water gushing over her head, bent over at the pump, alternating the pump handle with the simple soap weed, lye, and fat solution they made on the farm.

She had an oval face with unremarkable cheekbones or jawline, but two dimples that cheered the world when she could be convinced to laughter. Ever since the boyfriend debacle, she'd forsworn lipstick. Who saw her anyway, except Hazel? Travis, when she tended to him, thought she was old Aunt Ethel (who may or may not still be alive back east), so it truly didn't matter if she spent time on makeup or not.

Shelly preferred to wear a heavy denim set of work pants when she had anything at all to do outside. Still, after these 20-some years, she had a fear of rattlers that belied their scarcity on the property. She'd seen one, although she often heard them out past the edge of their hardscrabble garden. It was amazing that tomato plants grew out here; they always seemed a fussy plant. Shelly wore a series of soft cotton t-shirts that she washed every Saturday. She had one per day, and if she was feeling frisky, she'd alternate the colors week by week.

Still, she liked the simplicity and the routine of not worrying about what she looked like, how she presented herself, or who had what to say about her. She truly had no need to go out and see the rest of the world. She was in her 50s now, but still felt young and hale. Her hair had lost a lot of its sheen, and was about half gray. Her face had lines with tiny creases, but not frown lines. Not really smile lines, either, but simple lines that came with age and sun and work.

Chapter 3

Shelly and Hazel

The first few days, Shelly and Hazel tiptoed around each other, waiting to find safety. The next few weeks, they postured before they could find common ground. Then, finally, came the stable months and years that both Shelly and Hazel have long abided by—trusting things left unsaid, undiscovered, unchallenged. Travis had a lot to do with this last part—by nature, he had always been a peacemaker. His thin frame and stalwart spirit sketched out the living blueprint they all followed, sharing life together on Gladstone.

Hazel already knew that Shelly was pregnant when she stepped into the mercantile off the Trailways bus that day so long ago. Shelly thought she'd looked both confident and secretive, a young woman on her way to a new life. She fooled no one, except maybe the old drunk who sat in a stupor on the bus without acknowledging his surroundings. She certainly didn't fool the bus driver. He wagered, as soon as she stepped off the bus and walked into the mercantile, that she wouldn't want to continue.

"You know she ain't gettin back on that bus, don't you?" he'd said to Hazel when they stood at the front corner of the bus, negotiating the next delivery of whatever she'd needed 20 years ago.

"Yeah, I wondered about her," Hazel replied. "She does have that look in her eye."

"You ok to look after her for a few days? I'll be back eastbound in two days, and then I've got a westbound trip scheduled for Saturday," he said.

"So, worst case, she has to find herself in five days? I can swing that. I'll put her to work and let her see if this is the life she wants," Hazel said.

"Alright, then. It's always a pleasure talking to ya, Hazel. Do you think she wants her suitcase?" he asked.

"I'm guessing not. If she does, I'll put the flag out for you to stop on your eastbound trip, ok?"

"That'll do. That'll do just fine. You have a good day now, Hazel."

"Same to you, Ernie. Take good care."

At that, Hazel turned for the house, and Ernie walked back in front of the bus, pulled the door open, and settled himself heavily in the driver's seat. He'd left the bus running, but he ran a methodical check of all the other systems as he waited for the passengers to straggle back into the bus. The drunk had never gotten off. By the time Ernie got up to count heads, he was only one short. He blew a long blast on the air horn, waited a minute or two, and blew one more blast. After another long pause, he pulled the door lever shut, kicked in the clutch, and rolled out of the Gladstone drive.

Shelly, in due time, walked back to the main house. As she approached, she saw Hazel sitting on the back porch in a deep, tilted wooden chair. There was a tray on the table next to her, and an empty chair on the other side of the table. Two glasses sat on the tray.

"Would you like some iced tea?" Hazel asked.

"I—"

"It's ok. I know. I talked to the bus driver. He knows you're ok."

"I'm sorry. I just couldn't get on that bus again. That drunk guy smells so bad, and I just got afraid of..." She stopped talking without finishing.

"What's your name, sweetheart?" Hazel asked.

"Shelly. Just Shelly, if that's ok," she said.

"That's just fine, hon. That's just fine."

They sat in silence for several minutes. The only movement was the lifting and lowering of the glasses of tea. One mind whirled and trembled. One mind studied and quietened.

"So, I guess it's obvious, but I wonder if I could stay here? I mean, sleep here," Shelly said.

"Of course you may. My name is Hazel. It's just me and my Uncle Travis that live here."

"Oh. I wondered about that. I saw another house back there."

"Yes. Travis basically raised me since I was eight. He's ok. He doesn't talk much. But he's kind."

"I—I could work and stuff to help out, so I'm not a burden. I know how to do lots of chores," Shelly offered.

"Well, that's a welcome offer, Shelly. Travis and I pretty much split things down the middle. Anything outside he does, and everything inside I do."

"I can do either one. My father and mother," Shelly stopped as tears welled in her eyes. "My parents kept me hopping, that's for sure. They kicked me out, is all."

"Now, who in their right mind would kick out a young girl? What in the world did you do?"

"Well, that's just it. I didn't do anything. Or at least anything I had a choice in. But—"

"Yes?"

"Do you mind too awfully much if we don't talk about all that? I can scarcely understand it myself, and it makes me feel too stupid to try to explain it. It's why I didn't want to end up in whatever town the bus stopped at. Everyone's gotta know everybody's business."

"Of course. I totally understand," Hazel said briskly.

Hazel stood to her feet, brushed her skirt down, and smoothed her hair back off her forehead.

"Why don't you come with me? It's time to start the bread, and I could use some help. Would that be ok?"

The corners of Shelly's mouth turned up in a small smile. She rose to her feet, mimicking the skirt- and hair-straightening, and nodded her head to Hazel.

"I love fresh bread."

Chapter 4

Shelly and Hazel

The two women passed a quiet afternoon in the kitchen, working on baking several different loaves of bread, enough to last the three of them a few days. Hazel occasionally repeated what she was doing with flour, or yeast, or the few seasonings she threw in the mixing bowl, for the benefit of Shelly. It had taken on the feeling of a private cooking class. The bitter taste that had covered Shelly's tongue since she left Missouri had almost disappeared. She found herself cheerful as she watched the primitive yeast do the only thing it was good at: growing bubbles and eating sugar to make more bubbles. She was far too young to recognize the possibility of the allegory to her own life, but it cheered her, nevertheless.

"I used to have to bake this bread with a wood stove. I feel so spoiled having this gas stove; all I do is light the pilot light and set the temperature, and it stays there," Hazel said with delight.

"A wood stove to bake?" Shelly asked.

"Oh, sure—we had to cook on top of it and bake inside of it. It had a firebox over on the left side of the stove. I'd have to feed slats of wood into the firebox just right or else the bread would be burnt on one side and doughy on the other."

"How often did you ruin the bread?"

"Oh, Lord, when I was young it was almost half the time. But Travis and Nathan never complained. Well, they did. But not when they thought I could hear them. They'd sit out on the porch, after they said goodnight to me, and they'd kinda chuckle about it."

"Who is Nathan? Is he here, too?"

"Oh, no. Nathan left quite a few years ago. He was my uncle, too. My daddy's brothers."

"Ah. So, Travis is the only man here? You don't have a husband?" Shelly asked.

"Nope. Never really saw the point of one. And, yes, it's just been me and Travis for a while now."

Hazel showed her the room that she'd be staying in while she was at Gladstone.

She explained, "The Gladstone house is a long rectangle, with the mercantile front and center, the kitchen rear and center, and the four bedrooms pinning down one corner each. Pretty simple."

Hazel had taken the largest rear bedroom. The room to the right of the mercantile was where Hazel put extra stock and empty boxes, and the room to the left of the mercantile was full of sewing stuff. The rear bedroom on the left was clear, and this was the one that Hazel showed to Shelly.

"You take this one for now. It's got the best light."

It had a full mattress atop a homemade bed frame that had room underneath to shove a suitcase or shoes. The windows, one on each wall, had a layer of dust on the outside, so the slanting sun didn't feel too oppressive.

"It's lovely. What a welcome," Shelly said softly.

The blanket on the bed was a creamy color of cotton, and it had little pills of fabric either sewn onto it or knotted onto it. Two plump pillows sat in place, and a small rag doll reclined with its head at the junction of the pillows. The doll's long, floppy legs were crossed at the ankle; a jaunty, relaxed look. A small student desk sat in the inner corner of the room, old enough to contain a round hole for an inkwell and a channel for a pen or pencil that ran along the top edge of the desk. An oblong mirror sat above a chest of drawers that sat next to the desk. Those four things were the sum total of the decorating in the bedroom.

"Well? What do you think? I hope it will do," Hazel said with a smile.

"Oh my, yes. It's lovely. The sun in here in the morning will be super! My bedroom back home—" Shelly stopped.

"I mean, this will be great. Thank you more than I can even say. I just don't deserve any of it, but thank you."

"It's my pleasure, hon. Now why don't you—well, I was going to say unpack your things, isn't that funny?"

Shelly slipped her shoes off, turned a pirouette, lifted her hands, and said, "There. All unpacked!"

They giggled and flashed true smiles, both of them this time, at each other.

"Mess around a little bit and then come on back out. We'll go get Travis for supper. Ok?"

"Uh, sure. Is there, um, a bathroom somewhere?" Shelly asked.

"I totally forgot to show you that. Yes, absolutely there is a bathroom! It's in the center of the house between the mercantile side and the kitchen. There used to be but one wall as a divider, but then the uncles got fancy and built a second wall and put a bathroom in one half and a pantry in the other. You'll find it—a rectangle, you know," Hazel laughed. "Ok, see you soon."

"Thanks again, you don't even know…"

Chapter 5

Shelly and Hazel

Two hours later, Shelly awoke on the bed. Hazel had laid her hand gently on her shoulder to wake her. The light slanted in the window almost horizontally.

"How long was I out?"

"You're a tired young girl. That was almost two hours."

"Oof. I meant to stay up and help tidy things. Sorry about that," Shelly said.

"No apology necessary. Come with me to go meet Travis, ok?"

After a quick dash into the bathroom to pee and wash her face, Shelly and Hazel walked out the back door, across the wooden porch, and down the two steps to the dusty farm yard. This was the second time that Shelly had seen the back of the property, and the first sunset she'd seen in a place that wasn't her hometown ever. The bus had left her home stop before dawn, and driven the length of Kansas during the day. The stops must've been convenient to some other city, because the schedule sure wasn't convenient to her.

The cabin they approached looked almost as old as the Gladstone House. It could've used a fresh coat of paint, although the dark brown paint on there now may have been part of the problem. That shade and tint just looked plain old-fashioned. The trim was painted with the same heavy brown.

"He's usually on the back porch at sunset. Let's go around the side and check there first," Hazel said.

Feeling no need to reply, Shelly merely continued walking next to her. The air, she realized, wasn't heavy or sticky at all. It took no effort to walk through it. The temperature had cooled, and the air, too, had cooled. Most of her life so far had been a trudge through saturated, thick air that felt more like the heavy gravity of Jupiter (like she knew, she snorted to herself). A scent of wildness tinged the air she pulled in and out through her nose. She didn't know the names of the plants accenting it, but she wanted to learn. It was a joy to breathe. It was a joy to walk. A lightness of being unfamiliar to her.

Sure enough, around the corner, on another wooden porch, sat two rockers. One moving and occupied, the other empty. An older man in overalls smiled in the waning rays of sunlight painting the back wall of the cabin, the windows, and his shining eyes. She noticed he had a look of glacial permanence and serenity. Not flashy or noticeable or attention-getting, but sure that he'd seen wonder and glory before, and he would see it again.

"Welp, Uncle Travis, it's a big day!" Hazel said loudly.

"What's that?" the man said, cupping his hand behind his ear.

Hazel turned to Shelly. "You may as well know right now that he can't hear worth a darn. He sure can work all day, but don't bother calling for him."

"I said, it's a big day at Gladstone! We have a guest," Hazel said, stopping just short of shouting.

"I see that. She looks like a happy young woman. Is she a relative?" Travis said.

Shelly stepped forward, put one foot on the porch, and stuck out her right hand. "Hello, there. I'm Shelly," she said.

"Pleased ta meetcha," he said with a smile.

"I'm pretty sure we aren't related, sir, but I appreciate you letting me stay on."

"Oh, well, Hazel handles all that. If she says you can stay, then I say welcome," he said.

"Hey, smooth talker, how about you get up and come over for supper in about ten minutes? Shelly and I just need to finish up a few things, and we'll have the table set, ok?"

Shelly looked at Hazel with alarm, thinking there was way more prep that needed to be done than could be completed in ten minutes. Hazel merely patted Shelly's forearm and kept looking at Travis.

"Well, heck, I guess I'll have to quit doing what I'm doing and do that with you. I'll just make sure my hands are clean and then I'll head over to the house, for sure. And, after supper, Shelby, I'll take you on a quick tour of the place and show you all the stuff that Hazel avoids," he said benignly.

"I'd like that, Mr. Travis. See you for supper."

They waved back over their shoulders as they walked back towards the house, and watched the sun settle on the horizon, then sink slowly into it. Swifts flitted above their heads, chasing the bugs that took to the air upon dusk.

"You know I walked way back there on that road today? Do you guys own all that? Or is this it?" she asked.

"Oh, we own all that. Travis loves to talk about that. We'll get him spun up at supper and he can tell you all about it."

Chapter 6

Shelly and Hazel

"Now, Shelly, don't you stress over this bus driving up. I'll handle the counter; you can just stay in the kitchen," Hazel said, like a mantra, those first few weeks.

"That'd be great. If you need anything, I can hear you and come out," Shelly answered.

"I'll be fine. There's no one on this bus that can hurt you."

"You're right, I know. I don't know why it worries me every time."

The passengers mostly wanted to use the bathroom, buy a Coke, try the samples, and then buy a small gift bag of bread, jelly, or butter to take to whomever they hoped to see at the end of the bus trip.

After the bus had left, and Hazel had straightened the shop front and the counter, she came back into the kitchen. Shelly still sat at the table. Hazel sat down next to her.

"Are you worried that your parents will be on the bus? Is that it?"

"They'd never get on a bus and come look for me."

"But are you worried about it?"

Shelly sat for a minute, head down, lost in thought. A tear tracked down her face. Hazel took her hand, squeezed it for just a second. Then she let go and put her two hands in her lap.

Shelly looked up at Hazel. "I don't know how you can tell what's wrong without me even knowing."

"That's it, isn't it?"

"I think, yeah, I'm terrified my daddy will come looking, and, when he finds me, still disapprove of me."

"Do you think you should write to them?"

"I've thought about it. I just don't have any idea where I should start. I mean, how in the world could anything have changed?"

"Well, I bet they haven't moved. What would a letter back home hurt?" Hazel asked softly, like a person looking at a bunny in the backyard clover.

"I know. That makes me seem like the bad guy for leaving and never writing or calling. But I just can't forget his face when I left. He looked at me like I was rotten garbage. A roadkill skunk that he'd barely missed driving over on the highway."

"I thought you told me he told *you* to get out. No?"

"Yeah, that's what he said. 'Get out. Take your whoring ways with you.' And the worst of it is that Mama didn't even say anything to defend me."

"That isn't love, Shelly. That's judgment. Without grace. That does *not* make you the bad guy."

Shelly just sat and cried. She waved her hand once, faintly, like a fly had flown through her orbit.

"That makes you a survivor. And I'm so thankful you came here to survive. We'd be way poorer if you hadn't," Hazel said.

Hazel sat with Shelly while she—while they both—cried.

Shelly, years later, now sat on the back verandah of the Gladstone House. She sat back there because she didn't care to see any of the cars pass by. She didn't like waving to the little kids pressed against the windows, looking for anything worth talking about out here in eastern New Mexico.

"Don't you ever get tired or bored of this place, Shelly?" Hazel asked.

"I—no, is the short answer. I don't need a man, or a tour of the world. I need peace, is all," Shelly said.

Truth be told, the more time passed, the more she mourned for her little lost child that had never had a chance to grow into a baby. Shelly walked out to the ravine every now and then.

"Do you miss your baby?"

"Baby? You knew about that?"

"Oh, sweetheart, of course I knew. I knew the moment you missed that bus and stood there hoping I'd ask you to stay," Hazel said gently.

Shelly had stood there and wondered what her life might have been if she'd carried that little tyke to term. She could see the little girl (because she couldn't countenance another male on the property) gamboling around the dusty trails of this high desert, skipping past cholla, prickly pear, and yucca.

"I named her Amora," said Shelly. "I'm not sure that was a real name, but it had the Spanish word for love in it, anyway, which seems pure—like that tiny thing was."

Chapter 7

Travis

I walked back towards the house, plain tired out from the day's chores but also from carrying around that damned load of sadness for all these years. I stopped a second by the old cholla cactus, my favorite one. Favorite because it was there way back when I got here. I was just a kid. I don't think it's fair that I had to be the one. The decider.

"I was always better at letting things lie, than judging things," I said out loud.

No one out there to hear me. Agree or disagree. Lonely. That's what I am. That poor kid Hazel never did have a chance to have a normal childhood, what with no friends to play with. Plus all that constant work that her ma and pa did. Plus then her crazy uncle. Nathan. The one I had to put down. My brother.

"I sure as hell wish I woulda stayed back in Missouri. This here is probably the single worst decision I made. Even though I'd never leave her alone to undo it. Once we got here, it was too damned late to do anything else."

I shrugged a shoulder. Walked back to the house. Hoped for some supper. Hoped I wouldn't have to play my 'lost old man' character. I did that when they asked me the hard questions.

Chapter 8

Travis

Travis lived in a shotgun cabin that was on the east edge of the farm road on Gladstone. That cabin had originally been built for the brothers. There was a year there when James and Nathan thought a cattle drive up to La Junta was the answer to their problems. It was a long walk across eastern New Mexico and southern Colorado. At the time, that was the best place with the best chance of high prices for beef on the hoof, and they built the cabin for the cowboys they thought they'd hire to run the cattle. The brothers stopped driving beeves when they realized that other ranchers were trucking their cattle to market, and the market liked that beef, softened by feedlot living, more than they liked the gristly beef that they got with driven cattle.

Travis didn't mind the cabin; he had no need of air conditioning. He lived without it for all of his at-least-80 years, and didn't need it for these last few. Matter of fact, although he still rose with the sun and slept with the sun, he spent most of his time in one of two rockers in the cabin. One rocker sat facing west on his back porch. On a good day, he could see all the way to the line of mountains above Las Vegas and the Mora Valley. The other rocker sat in his front room and faced north. On any day there, he could see the Rabbit Ears Mesa and the Capulin Volcano. He still hoped one day to see that volcano blow, even though his last teacher, Miss Janet, told him that the volcano was from way back when, was dormant, and would never blow again. He told her then, and still believed to this day, that it would. He just knew it.

Occasionally, when Hazel came in to check on him, he mumbled something about Capulin to her. She'd just pat his hand and agree that it could blow at any second.

"I'd sure love to see that, too, Travis. Don't give up on it now."

Travis would lift his head from its slumber on his chest, and smile a sunny, carefree smile at her.

"Thanks for lookin' after me, Hazel."

He'd usually get her name right. Sometimes she was Ethel (a long-lost aunt), sometimes it was actually Shelly that came to tend to him (he rarely noticed—and Shelly doubted he actually knew her name), and sometimes it was that girl he loved who, during his last year of schooling, was in the eighth grade—Julie. It didn't matter, though. Travis was docile and mostly continent. The women guessed he got up and used the privy without any prompting and little help from them. And if they had to occasionally re-button his shirt or help zip his trousers, he paid them no mind, and caused them no ill thought when they did it.

Back in the day when his daddy's admonition to keep a cottonwood planted was still fresh in his mind, he sat in the shade of the old cottonwood and had a thought. He noticed, as he looked up, that there was a deep groove in the lowest branch off the trunk. That branch shot out at an angle from the trunk, not horizontal but way shallower than 45 degrees, and the shallowest angle of all the other branches of the cottonwood. The other branches, too, were as much as 25 feet up the trunk, so this one snaked alone out into the fresh air. The groove, not a scar so much as a channel, appeared to be a healthy part of the tree. If it had been used constantly for a long time, the bark would have been sawn through by whatever made the groove, and that same branch would have died. An infrequent use, then, but enough to stop the bark from growing over the groove like a scab would.

"Now what in the world would Granddaddy and Uncle be using this tree for? Maybe slaughtering an animal?"

In his confusion, he didn't realize his question put two vastly different timelines right next to each other to make one. Had Travis been able to peer into the past and back in Missouri, he would've seen the animals that got butchered by his granddaddy and his uncle, neither of whom made the trip to Gladstone. He would also have seen that, here on Gladstone, it was the 'bad seed' brother that did the slaughtering, and that a few of the animals had driven their own cars onto the property—destined never to leave.

Chapter 9

Travis

Travis transplanted a new cottonwood right next to the old one. The volunteer seedlings grew with no order, so Travis moved them around to suit.

"You'll want to tend the grove of cottonwoods going around the spring," his brother had said. "Not too many, and let a new one or two keep growing. Just in case the old ones take sick or get blown over. Important for the ritual."

But Travis's older brother had died before he ever trusted to tell him what the ritual was.

"Died, hell. I killed him. I had to," he muttered to himself. "If I hadn't-a done that, I'd a been long gone, Hazel'd been long gone. None-a this would be around, leastways not in any way I could recognize."

Travis scuffed back to the main house, thinking it was just about time for lunch and hoping the girls had put something together.

"Those hogs are the only thing I've ever seen that eat more than I do," he said as he entered the back door into the dining room.

"Well, hey there, Travis. Just in time for lunch," Shelly said.

A flicker of relief crossed his face when he heard this—truth be told, he got pretty confused pretty easily lately.

"I figured it was lunch time, but am glad to be right about that!" he said with a smile. No need to tell the woman speaking to him that he wasn't sure what her name was anymore.

"Travis, did you remember to milk the cows yesterday afternoon? Opal was busy with Claire, and you said you'd do it?" Hazel asked.

"Of course. I never forget a cow," he crowed.

In truth, he had no earthly idea what he'd done yesterday afternoon. The cows seemed fine this morning, though, so he must've done it.

The spring that the cottonwoods grew next to never dried up. Not even in the worst of the 30s, when even the creek that usually ran with winter runoff never filled up. That's when they got their water from the spring. He kept busier than normal those few years because the stock were always thirsty and the windmill didn't always have water to pull from the ground—that's how low the water table had gotten.

Travis lived through the Depression as a teenager, already done with schooling (he'd made it through the sixth grade, which was plenty back then) and been on the Gladstone Ranch as free family labor. His brother, who was Hazel's father, had no wish to expand or sell. They just wanted to keep living right there, with as little contact with the outside world as possible. They realized that the few travelers that stopped there were necessary to make a few dollars so they could buy the things that barter didn't work for.

James and Nathan, his brothers, didn't bother to tell Travis to be careful when he wandered or rode across the property. Travis knew what animals and plants were dangerous. If he died by snakebite, that was his own fault, and he knew James and Lily would bury him just like he buried the idiot sheep that broke their necks trying to jump a ravine that was too wide. "Damned fool woulda died some way or another," he'd say. And Travis knew he'd say the same of him if it happened.

James warned him about things, but it was more along the lines of snow or thunderstorms or lightning. Or cows about to calve ("those bitches get *way* meaner than bulls"), or bulls who've got the scent of a cow in them ("they're crazy and won't stop for nothin'"). Travis had the run of the property, but tried all kinds of ways to avoid the arroyo.

"I get an odd feeling when I walk out there, Hazel," he said to his niece.

"I understand. I don't feel the same way, but I can see how you'd get the shivers out there," she'd said. "I've always kinda liked the spring, myself. Just sitting next to it. For what that's worth."

Chapter 10

Nathan

Nathan, brother to James and Travis and uncle to Hazel, saw the world in a way that stripped all people of their posturing. He believed he could see into each person's soul and know their true intent. He felt a call from the Lord Almighty to rid the world—at least his corner of it—of the people who only had ill will and a lust for mayhem and wrongdoing. Few were called to this, he believed. He counted himself as a Knight Templar, or a Crusader, or even an Avenging Angel.

His grandfather, also named Nathan, quietly showed him the way to rid the world of cancerous people and how to dispose of the evidence. Nathan took this spore with him when he and Travis traveled west to live with James and Lily.

"Don't tell anyone else about this," old Nathan had said. "The little people—the *blind* people—of this world will not understand our calling to make this a better place. That's why we don't tell what we've done to cull the world of the cancer, which is growing all the time."

"Yes, Grandpa. I believe you," Nathan said, entranced by his zeal.

Nathan was a sponge. He absorbed—that's all he knew. He had no idea that what he pulled from his grandfather was toxic. He had no thought as to how that poison would out itself many years, and many miles, later.

His mother and father didn't realize that Grandpa Nathan had taken a plunge off the deep end, and just thought the intergenerational relationship was serendipitous, and meaningful, and a loving story of heritage. Mother and Father would realize it when they had problems with Grandfather Nathan, but they were too far away, and too late to salvage Young Nathan. Even if they had thought to warn James, Lily, or Travis, it was not soon enough to stop the killing. Mother and Father were relieved that all the children were gone, and safe in New Mexico.

Young Nathan learned from Grandpa Nathan how to throw the thick hemp rope over the limb, settle the rope in the groove, stretch the legs of the victim on a stick driven between the ankle bone and the Achilles tendon, and tie the rope to the stick. In the dark of night, once every few years during a new moon, the body tugged high enough so he could stand under it. The first cut across the throat of the victim, a pause to wash, to revel in, a gush of blood from still-pumping heart, then the careful dissection into unrecognizable parts of a body. Like Grandpa Nathan, the joy was in the coppery smell while cutting, and neither of them felt an urge to consume or taste or cook. Ridding the world of the cancer, that was the call. That was enough. And if, perhaps, a human victim slipped in there on occasion, more's the better, the lesson taught.

Nathan, upon arriving at Gladstone and surveying the property, found that the old cottonwood, halfway between the spring and the first house, was a perfect place to continue the ritual—the one thing he brought with him, the hanging and bleeding of a carcass. In a pinch, the windmill would work, too. Nathan figured he'd need options, sooner or later, to do his part in the cleansing.

Nathan returned to his obsession with spiritual prophecy like a marble swirling down a drain. No matter where his conversation started, he veered towards the coming tribulation surely as water seeks the lowest level. He couldn't help but abjure, caution, warn, urge whatever listener he had captive that they needed to seek the Lord's face and favor right now, before it was too late. His heart was probably in the right place, but the mechanics of any conversation were so exhausting that the listener almost always resorted to monosyllabic agreement just to get to the end of the interaction. He never noticed them edging away from him as he became more strident.

"Really? I hadn't heard that," the listener might say.

"You haven't heard because the Lord hasn't revealed it to you," Nathan would say.

"I hear your words, and will think about them."

"You'd best do more than think on them. You'd be wise to drop your superficial yearnings and go to the Lord in prayer. On your knees. With no shoes on," Nathan would grind out. "You have no idea how bad it will get."

One day, when Nathan was showing Travis how to care for the hogs—"This is the last time I'm gonna show you, I swear"—and they found one of the animals bleeding, Travis noticed Nathan breathing heavily with glazed eyes.

"What the hell's wrong with you, Nathan?"

Nathan shook himself, dragged his gaze back to Travis. "I'll thank you not to curse, young brother. There's nothing wrong with me."

"It sure looks like you're about to pass out."

"Nothing that a little butchering won't cure. I think that there hog is too far gone to doctor back to health. You agree?" Nathan said.

"That one? Hell, that's just a scratch from a bit of wrestlin' between 'em for food. There's no reason to butcher anything!"

"That goes to show you how very, very little you know about the ways of infection, little brother. I say we set up the butcher pot this afternoon. Before she turns septic," Nathan replied.

"I say you're a crazed idiot. Lemme just get the fixin' cream out and slop some on her. She'll be fine," Travis grunted, then stood abruptly to his feet and backed out of the barn.

He was spooked enough from the encounter that he never did get the cream. Didn't go back to the hog barn.

"You do that, little brother. Then we'll see," Nathan said, keeping his eyes on the sow like a laser. Like a mountain lion. Like a predator.

The next morning, when Travis returned to the hog barn to check on that sow, he couldn't find her. He followed the drag marks out the door, along the track, and to the cottonwood. Under the groove, the blood had curdled into a black scab on the dirt. Ants had started to carry away the clots. The heavy manila rope was coiled and lay at the base of the trunk, stained with fresh blood. Neither the carcass nor Nathan was there; and when Nathan came back, nearly two days later, stinking and dirty, they didn't pass one word about it.

Never did, in fact.

Chapter 11

Travis

I knew right then we were in a heap of trouble. That damned sow musta weighed 300 pounds, and Nathan walked off with it. I got no desire to find out what he done with it, either. He didn't go sell it in town, though, that's for certain. Right then is when I started watchin' him every minute, just waitin' for him to decide that one a *us* was too sick or wounded to continue on, and he needed to stop the infection before it got outta hand.

Chapter 12

Springer

Of course, the farm had always needed supplies, even back when it was just Travis and Hazel. After the parents and Nathan were gone; before Shelly, Opal, and Claire showed up. It usually fell on a Thursday when Travis and Hazel drove into town. They took the old truck. It had a full-sized bed with wood rails on each side. They could load it down until the springs creaked in protest, but, in truth, they rarely needed that much stuff on a weekly basis. One of the times, though, they decided they could take a load of pigs in for the Thursday market and bring back a load of feed for the animals along with winter supplies of staples. Hazel usually drove in, and Travis usually drove back. This time, Travis drove both ways because of the load.

"They'll shift around on you when you don't expect it, Haze," he said. "I wouldn't want that on my conscience, is all."

"I've driven that truck nearly as much as you have, Travis, but it's fine. You can be in charge. They always think you are, anyway."

"True. Cuz I'm a real cowboy," he bellowed in a laugh.

His laugh was contagious. He started in on his 'real cowboy' routine which pulled Hazel out of whatever funk she found herself that day. He'd strut around with his hat in his hand, gesturing wildly around him and talking in a grandiose way about "my ranch out on the high plains." As if there were an audience of rapt New Yorkers who'd never seen a wide open sky with streaks of thin, pure white cloud accenting a day. City people who wouldn't know how to get coffee without someone to serve it to them, even if they were standing right next to a hot wood stove with a potful sitting on top.

"Step right up, you city people, and come see a real live cow! They actually exist and we have several captured in this here building that we call a barn!"

Hazel would hold her sides and spin in gleeful circles, then she'd pretend she was a wide-eyed city girl.

"What did you call these again?" she'd ask in a dimpled, awestruck voice.

"These here is cows, ma'am. C-O-W-S. Have you ever tried butter? Or cheese?"

"Why, yes, sir, Mr. Cowboy, I surely have. Don't tell me that this here cow is part of that?" she said as she pretended to almost faint and fan her face.

"The very thing, madam. We just squeeze this cow's… *teat*," he said, whispering the word, "and out comes butter or cheese, whichever the cow wants to give us."

"Can it make Gruyère or blue cheeses, too?"

Travis would stop, scuff the dirt, take his hat off his head, and try not to laugh when he said, "Well, no, miss. We'd need a French cow for that. And all's we have is plain old American cows. So we only get Colby or Cheddar."

"Ah, that's a shame," Hazel would say in her city-girl voice.

Then they'd collapse against each other in laughter, staggering back towards the house, or the truck, or whatever chore they had next on their list. It was a sunny time on the farm—which they'd recently started calling the Gladstone Project. Travis drove the truck back to the pig building, backed right up almost to the door, and then propped the doors open so there was no way around the truck and out into freedom. He slid a wooden ramp into place with one end on the tailgate and one end on the ground. The ramp had small strips of wood screwed horizontally every eight inches or so to help the pigs keep traction when they finally trotted up the ramp.

Hazel, with her rubber muck boots on, shooed a dozen yearling pigs out of the main compartment in the barn, and then stood in the gateway so they couldn't turn back around and run into a corner of the pen. Travis looked at the group carefully, then selected nine of them to run up the ramp and into the truck bed. The other three, he said, they'd keep for next spring or maybe even the winter. He nodded once to Hazel and she stepped aside so they could wander back into the pen. Hazel spoke some words, most of them meaningless, in a calm tone that let the pigs know the hassle was over for the day and they could go back to sleeping in the mud, like usual. Travis had slung the ramp up into the bed and shut one barn door, waiting on her to come out to shut the other. He latched it and climbed back into the cab. Before he did, he took off his muck boots while Hazel took off hers, and they both put them in the slot between the truck cab and the truck bed, upside down so the soles faced up. No sense getting pig shit all over the floor of the cab.

Travis made a three-point turn on the road and headed for the highway. He stopped, looked carefully both ways, then eased onto the westbound lane towards Springer. Hazel turned the knob on the old Delco radio, spinning the dial to see if there was more than one station since they last drove in.

"You know there's only the one station, Hazel. Why do you keep checking?"

"You don't know. Some fancy New Yorker could've moved out here and wanted to bring some actual music to us little people!"

"Not this week, I guess. Same old preacher telling us how bad we are and how much worse it's going to get."

"Yeah. Dang."

Chapter 13

Springer

They drove in silence the rest of the two hours. As they got to the outskirts of Springer, the load of pigs in the back started to agitate, stepping to one side or the other of the bed, oinking loudly.

"They smell the auction, don't they?"

The wind was coming off the mountains still west of them, and Travis and Hazel could smell hogs on the breeze. They drove straight through town, under the interstate, and out west where the livestock auction sat. The auction had several a week, but Thursdays was always hogs. Big hogs, little hogs, mama hogs, piglets, shoats, sows, boars; healthy first, then a few sick stragglers that always seemed to have a buyer. Travis drove onto the lot, around to the rear, then got in the short line of trucks to drop off their load. It wasn't more than a ten-minute wait in line before they pulled up to the small hut where the intake crew kept track.

"Well, hey there, Travis. Haven't seen you in a while! Hello, Hazel, how do you do?" Anthony said. Anthony had worked the auction for years, one of his myriad jobs that kept ranchers hopping.

"You feel like selling these few hogs for us today?"

"Hell, yeah, we'd be happy to. Matter of fact, we got a few buyers that come all the way down from Pueblo, for some reason, so we oughta be able to get a damned fair price for these bast—uh, these here hogs for you," Anthony said, sliding a look at Hazel right after he changed the wording of the sentence. Hazel smiled and waved her hand in a dismissive, conciliatory gesture at him.

"Now, Anthony, you know I've heard you cuss before. It doesn't bother me one little bit! I know you'll take care of our tiny little cash crop and get us a real good deal," she said lightly.

"We sure will, ma'am, and that's a promise."

The boys at the back of the truck had already boxed the bed in with the fence and gates, had slid the ramp in place, and, after the spryest of the auction help had jumped up into the bed, herded them down the ramp and towards a holding pen for appraisal and later sale.

"Here's your claim ticket, Travis. Nine yearlings, spotted black and white, mixed sex. We'll get them sorted and sold; we'll see you later today when you come back. We've got about 1400 to sell, so should be done by three p.m. or so, ok?"

"Sounds good, Anthony. Stay outta trouble now, for once," Travis joked as he put the truck in gear and pulled away.

Anthony waved and had already turned to the next pick-up in line as they pulled out of the drop-off row.

Chapter 14

Springer

They drove back into town, parked in front of the gas station, where he turned the truck off to fill it up. Hazel stepped out, stretching her arms out wide. She looked over at the side of the station at the bench that ran along the wall. She made eye contact with the old man that, at least every time she was in town, sat there soaking up the sun while hardly moving. She walked over close, but not right up to the bench. The man opened his eyes and looked at her.

"Hola, Hazel. ¿Cómo le va?" he said.

"Luís. How are you? May I sit?" she returned.

"Of course. The bench is here for you, too," he said.

They'd greeted each other this way for several years, and had taken for granted that they'd sit and talk for a few minutes whenever she came around. She'd sit and talk with him, whether it was just her or if Travis came along—it didn't matter. Luís was an old Native from the Mora Valley, he'd told her. He'd moved up north to Springer because his son and daughter-in-law bought the gas station and tiny general store that came together, here on one of the main corners in town. There were more gas stations one exit up, at the north end of Springer, for all the travelers on the interstate, but all the local people came and got their gas here. Cheaper, usually by about a dime. Plus, the daughter-in-law sold tamales out of a glass food warmer inside that were well worth the trip in their own right.

"How's it going? Out there on the high scrub. At your project?" Luís asked, using one twitch of each index finger to acknowledge Gladstone.

"Oh, gosh. I'm not sure. Of anything. I'm not sure it's worth the hassle, or the work, or the sweat, or the money."

"It will be, though. It's a long-term project, right? None of those make sense this early."

"Yeah. I keep hearing you tell me that. But who's the long-term project for? I mean, it's just us right now."

"You'll find someone to care about. You can't rush that," Luís said.

"You say that. But neither one of us wants to work at finding a person or people or whatever to come out there and stay. Where are we gonna look?"

Luís and Hazel sat for a minute, watching Travis top off both tanks in the truck, check the oil, kick the tires. Satisfied, Travis walked slowly towards the building, waving at

Luís as he went inside to pay. Travis came out a minute later, his hands full. One hand held a paper plate with tamales on it, and the other hand had a brown paper bag.

"Here ya go, Hazel. Have a tamale—I'm starved so I got us double the usual. Luís, I'd be happy to go back in and get you a few?" he asked.

"Naw, thanks, Travis. I just ate. Just finishing my coffee and enjoying the suntan," he replied.

"What's in the bag? Or do I have to ask?" Hazel said.

"Well, heck, she'd just wrapped a fresh batch and they smelled so good and we are gonna have to eat dinner tonight, aren't we?"

They shared a laugh. Hazel scooted closer to Luís so Travis could sit down. They picked at the tamales, steam rising from them when they broke one open.

"I was just telling Hazel here that you don't need to worry about finding someone to appreciate your 'ranch project'," Luís leaned forward and said to Travis.

Travis looked at him, tipped his straw hat back to rub his forehead, and sat back on the bench.

"We've been kinda wonderin' about that. I should be surprised you know, but I'm not after all these years. You have a sense about these things, Luís," Travis mused.

"Oh, I don't think it's anything special. I can just tell how you two are when you pull up. Hazel looks worried, is all."

"I do not! I'm perfectly fine. You can stop worrying about me," she said stoutly.

"Of course. Pardon me," he said, smiling. "But still, you don't need to worry. You know why?"

Travis and Hazel just looked at him, knowing that he'd continue speaking. Travis shrugged one shoulder.

"The reason you don't have to worry is that there's already someone, somewhere, who needs out of what they have. And they need a fresh start somewhere. You guys—your 'project'—is going to be that answer."

"We've started calling it the 'Gladstone Project'—did I tell you that last time?" she asked.

"Oh, really? The Gladstone Project, huh?" He worked the phrase over slowly, rubbing his chin. "I like it. Sounds pretty fancy, but you know that, right? Part of the attraction, right?"

Travis just laughed, nodding his head in agreement.

"I'm so glad you approve, Señor Luís," Hazel chuckled back at him.

After a few more minutes of conversation, they wished him a good day and continued on to the next destination, where they first sluiced out the bed of the pickup, then filled it level with the metal sides with different bags of feed for the livestock. At the mercantile, they slung a large bag of flour and smaller bags of rice and potatoes on top of the feed bags. A last stop at the fresh grocery market for typical but humble ranch and farm food made the truck almost as weighed down as when they drove in. They headed back to the livestock auction to collect their earnings, then immediately stopped at the bank to deposit most of the money, keeping just a little of it. The drive back home brought a serenity to them that had eluded at least Hazel earlier that morning.

"Do you think he's right?" she asked.

"Luís? Yeah. He usually is. I don't know how he does it, but he knows stuff like that."

"I hope so. Otherwise, what's it all for?" she said.

Chapter 15

Opal and Claire

Opal had the baby with her when she showed up on the doorstep of Gladstone. Opal said she came from the other side of Taos, and had left a bad situation, and that "she didn't want to talk about it." Opal asked if she could stay awhile and work for her keep.

"I don't eat much, and this here baby is a good one. She hardly cries and won't stop me from working."

"What's your baby's name?" Hazel asked.

"Well, I guess I'm thinking of naming her Claire," Opal said.

"You haven't named her?"

"I guess not. I've been waiting to see what name fits her," Opal said, not wanting to admit that she'd only decided to keep her after fleeing from her boyfriend's threat to give it (his word) away.

"That makes sense. What's the hurry, right?"

Hazel had smiled.

Opal and Claire, once they decided to stay, lived in the back room of the main Gladstone House. Although the house faced north and its width ran parallel to the highway, the back room where Opal stayed had great windows that faced both south and west. She could see the storms whipping up at the edge of the mountains, and she loved to rock Claire and watch the storms advance towards her, lightning marking the progress. The air was so dry here in Gladstone that the storms rarely had enough fury left to do more than cast some virga. Barely settled the dust.

One morning, after Opal had just arrived, Hazel woke to a pall of smoke coming through her doorway. It smelled like grease with a burnt plastic and coffee chaser. She sat up quickly, scuffed her feet into her slippers, and stepped into the kitchen without fixing her hair or putting a robe on. Opal was turning this way and that in the kitchen, a wild look in her eye while she waved her hands around, trying to get the smoke out of the fully open window.

"The kitchen's not your gift, is it, Opal?"

"I was trying to make breakfast for all of you," she said. "This stove got away from me."

"It takes a gentle touch to get the stovetop burner set just right. Looks like you got the grease a mite too hot for those, uh, pancakes, were they?" Hazel asked.

"That was the plan, yeah. And the coffee pot—how do you screw up *coffee?*"

"That there isn't a stovetop coffee pot. That's the one that plugs into the electricity. Pretty sure you've done melted it into not much use."

"I never learned much about cooking, I guess," Opal admitted.

"Let me show you how to make coffee the stovetop perk way. Looks like we'll be drinking our coffee that way, anyway, for a while."

"I'm so sorry!"

"Oh, gosh, not at all. I *like* this kind of coffee—it's a nice change," Hazel said. "Don't you worry one second about all this. Just set the skillet on the cutting board here for a minute and let it cool down. Here's the coffee pot. See how the inner basket and chimney thing come out?"

Opal gripped the smoking cast-iron skillet with both hands, a towel wrapped around the handle, the tomato seeds on the cutting board sizzling.

"Yeah, I do. That doesn't look so mystical."

Hazel laughed. "No mystery at all. After all, they made these so ranch hands could get coffee hot and quick before a full day of work, so it can't be that difficult to figure out.

Fill the pot with water, put the basket thing back in, dump some coffee in the basket."

Opal began to spoon coffee towards the basket, haphazardly, the hunted look still on her face.

"Easy now. *Only* in the basket—if coffee gets in the water, then it'll pour out into our cups. That's good enough for a campfire, but no good for our fancy Gladstone House, right?" she said.

"Right. That makes sense, Hazel," Opal said, with a fragile smile, and took a breath.

The spring on the back screen door twanged as it opened, followed by Shelly kicking the toes of her boots on the top step to knock the desert off.

"Whoa! What happened in here, girls?" she said.

"We got a little carried away cooking this morning. We didn't want you to go hungry, Shelly," Hazel said, arching a brow at her as she half-nodded towards Opal.

"Ah," Shelly paused, taking her hat off and setting the basket of just-picked produce on the counter. "It's a good thing, too, that you've thought about my hunger—I'm famished! I'll eat anything."

"I burned it all," Opal said.

"Nonsense. These cakes look perfect; I like them a little high brown. And, I do believe I read somewhere that the scorch is good for your system. Sign me up," Shelly said.

"You don't have to eat all this burned stuff, Shelly. I'm going to cook a second round; Hazel said she'd help me figure it out better."

"Alright, then, I'll wait, you smooth talker. How about some coffee?"

"I burned that, too," Opal said.

At that, Shelly tipped her head back and laughed delightedly, flowing out of her and into both of the other women in the kitchen. Hazel giggled like a much younger version of herself, and Opal, uncertainly, smiled then laughed outright.

Soon enough, the new coffee was burbling, and a fresh cast-iron skillet of cakes, browned just right and plated, had them all smiling.

Chapter 16

Opal and Claire

After breakfast, Hazel took her out to the pigs and cows when Travis was out there caring for them. He showed her what needed to be done every day. Opal felt at home with the animals, and was thankful that she wouldn't need to keep trying to learn how not to burn food on the stovetop or in the oven. Opal ate, but she never gave a care about what it was that she ate, or how it was prepared, or how much of it she got. She ate when she was hungry, and was just as happy with a crust of bread as she was with a fine roast and potatoes on a Sunday. In point of fact, she was often surprised when the full table was set and Travis came in to eat with them for Sunday dinner.

"I'll be honest, I'd much prefer to stay inside here and help with the kitchen than go out there and get dirty taking care of animals and plants every day," Shelly said. "Feel like working outside, Opal?"

"I'll pull my weight wherever you two say, but if I never have to cook again, I'll be pretty danged happy," Opal said. "Yeah, show me what to do."

"Let's go see if Travis is around; he can give you the whole tour."

Opal set up the sling for baby Claire, pushed her chair in, and followed Shelly out the door. Sure enough, they found Travis out in the hog barn, leaning against a center pole and watching them eat.

"That speckled one there don't seem like he's eatin' too good, does he, Shel?" Travis said.

"Travis, this is Opal and Claire. Do you remember they came to stay with us for a while?" Shelly said. "When you're done out here, we left a big plate of breakfast for ya."

"Pleased to make your acquaintance, Opal. And this tiny thing is Claire?"

He stuck one finger near her chubby fist and waited as she gripped it. He wiggled his finger around with her fist around it, both of them smiling. Opal looked at Shelly, one eyebrow questioning because they'd already been introduced more than once to him. Shelly smiled back at her but gave her head a half-shake.

"Travis, they want to help with the animals," Shelly said. "Do you think you can show them what they could do to help you?"

"I'd be happy to! Why just the other morning, I was layin' there in bed wishin' I didn't have to come out here and check on these danged cows," he said. "And thanks in advance for breakfast; I'm sure I'll love it."

"We can show them the cows, too, Travis. Do you want to tell them about the pigs first since they're right here?"

"Good idea. Yeah, the hogs are pretty simple. They want to sleep and eat. Here's where we keep all the feed, and I guess I shovel out the pens once or twice a week, don't I, Shel?"

"It's probably about that, yeah. Why don't you show her how to latch the doors so they can't get out?" Shelly said.

They walked over to the main double barn doors, which he'd swung open and left open. They all stepped outside, and he swung them shut.

"The thing is, if you don't latch this when you close 'em, and then *put this bent nail through like a stopper*, those danged hogs will nudge at the doors and work 'em free 'til they can push on out. Then they'll make a mess of things for sure."

"Ok, I'll be sure to remember the bent nail trick. Do they run off, then?"

"Hell, they don't run too far… they get hungry and come back. But they'll dig up all kinds of stuff we have planted, they'll go and try to wreck the foundation of the barn, and they'll make holes right in the road."

Travis pushed both his hands into his back, bent backwards, and grimaced up at the sky. He stood straight, his jaw slack. Opal looked at Shelly. Shelly shrugged one shoulder slightly, motioned toward the road with her chin. The two women with one tiny baby walked back towards Gladstone House, waiting to talk.

"He does that?"

"He does. He's fine; I've stood and waited many times to make sure he isn't going to fall or get lost or hurt himself. He usually just gives his head a shake and looks around. Then he picks up right where he left off," Shelly said.

"You don't get him to snap out of it?" Opal asked.

"It's easier to just let him be. I've done it, sure. But he gets agitated and mad, so it's no fun. He always acts like it's my fault. Plus, he forgets all about it day to day, anyway, so what's the point?"

"Well, I guess that makes sense."

"I'm going to walk on back to the house. Do you want to come with, or stay out here a while?" Shelly asked.

"I think we'll walk around out here for a minute, if that's ok," Opal said.

Opal turned back away from Gladstone House, looked down the road, and decided to see how far that went. Claire still sat happily in the sling, looking out with wide eyes. Opal walked as far as the ravine, marveling at the erosion along the sides and the depth of the channel.

"Must be some fierce rainstorms to keep this channel like this, huh, Claire?"

Opal backtracked along the road, noticing the foot trail that led off to the right of the road. She stepped onto the trail, walking the slight rise, then down the other side of the grade. The trail slid to the right, around a small mound, which concealed the sheltered shallow bowl of the spring that seeped out of the low sandstone berm at the far edge of the bowl.

"Did they tell us there was a spring out here, Claire? I don't think so."

She sat, unslung the baby, and propped against her shins. There were a few large stones that rimmed the edge of the bowl. Opal had perched on one of these. The sun was bright and warm. A fleet of three dragonflies buzzed the surface of the pool, then swung near the two girls before racing off around the backside of the mound. Opal felt a safety here, next to the seeping spring. She picked Claire back up, stretched her legs out, and breathed a sigh.

"Even though I forget what day it is out here sometimes, I think we're safe. Don't you, Claire?"

Claire, still a baby, just gurgled.

Chapter 17

Travis

She just looked so damned much like Hazel when she was younger! I would've started cryin' like all get out if I hadn't-a done my 'stand and stare' routine. I ruined Hazel, that's for sure. All's she wanted was a chance at a girlhood—as it was, the blood she carried around on her soul was more than a person should have to bear.

My fault. All of it.

Chapter 18

Hazel

Hazel didn't mind being in charge of the Gladstone Project, as she called it. She didn't call it that out loud, of course. When young Shelly showed up, Hazel had told her to call it the Gladstone House, as if it were a great fortress or plantation on the high desert. Hazel had to think of something, though, because that young girl was so forlorn, and obviously pregnant, that Hazel didn't want to turn her away—lest she take the bus all the way to Las Vegas and get sucked into some unwholesome solution to a young girl's life.

Sitting with the Opal and Claire, Hazel said, "I never went out to my parents' graves. They had died back in the 30s, when most of the country was in the grip of the Great Depression. The Great Depression wasn't much of a thing out here in Gladstone—the Dust Bowl, now that was a problem for us. I'd been a youngster at the time, and words like penniless, starving, hopeless, despairing, didn't mean much to any of us."

A pause. Opal and Claire waited.

"My father, James, had always said, 'These people don't know a good thing when they see it.' I figured that he meant something like living in Gladstone meant they were self-sufficient and didn't need to depend on fake fortunes buying and selling crop futures or bank shares, but he was always saying stuff like that, and I was pretty young to follow it all."

"How long did you go to school?" Claire said, then, turning to her mother with alarm, asked, "I don't have to go to school, do I, Mama?"

"Well, you will. You just haven't yet. We gotta figure that out, don't we?" Opal replied to her, then shifted her attention back to Hazel.

"I finished the sixth grade, over in Springer, and had then come home to live for good. I worked hard every day, just like my parents did, but so what? That's what a girl does. And, when my parents took sick and died, I took over the property and worked even harder to make sure it still flourished."

"Why wasn't it Travis who took over?"

"Oh, I guess we both did it. I don't know; I guess I always felt like I had to make the hard decisions. Ever since I was a girl."

"That sounds exhausting," Opal said.

"It was. It is. But..." Hazel shrugged.

Hazel was pretty sure she was 75. She might've been a year younger or older, give or take. She was five when the Great Depression finally wended its way to eastern New Mexico, and eight when her parents died. It wasn't like she had to run the *entire* project by herself, of course. Her Uncle Travis did most of the heavy lifting and work. He made it *seem* like she was a critical part of the success of the operation, though. In a way, that gave her purpose and joy.

"You know, we shot what food we needed," Hazel said to Opal.

"I didn't know that. But I'm not surprised," Opal answered.

"A slinking coyote is never good news for a small ranch operation," Hazel declared. She glared out at the prairie, daring one to come into view.

They sat and rocked for a minute.

Opal remarked, "Hazel, aren't you hot in that full skirt?"

"Oh, I'm used to these. It's what I've worn for almost ever."

She'd stitched a number of them over the years, and when one wore out, she'd send away for another bolt of material to make a few more. The bus took her order to town, and brought the cloth back a week or two later.

"Did you ever drive the truck into town?" Opal asked.

"Used to. All the time—once a week. It wasn't like I couldn't drive the old truck into town now; it would most likely make the trip. I've done it. Travis and I have done it. But…"

But then she'd have to make sure the fuel in the old farm tank was still stable, and she kind of forgot how to use the kit that measured fuel stability. On a good day, Travis could show her. That wasn't worth the risk, especially when the Trailways stopped every second or third day. The skirts were always pure cotton. They washed the best. And they dried quickly. She used the skirts as a dish towel for her hands, because it was easier than wearing an apron. Or actually carrying a dish towel.

"One of the few things I remember my mother teaching me was how to sew this frill onto my collars," Hazel said. "I still love them."

She smoothed her wiry gray hair back into a bun, or sometimes into a low ponytail. This day, it was in a freshly shaped and tamed bun. A black ribbon tied it close to her head in the back, and kept it from escaping. She liked to have her hair and clothes just so—it helped her pretend to keep a handle on what was important in her life.

"Did you ever love someone? Meet someone? Get engaged?" Opal asked.

"Oh, well, I don't suppose I ever did. I'm not sure what's wrong with me about that."

Hazel sat, lost in thought, and remembered that she loved a woman once. The time that Esther came through and stayed a few weeks made Hazel realize that she wasn't the same as the other girls she'd known.

Esther had gotten up once in the middle of the night to get a drink of water. Hazel heard her, had risen from her own bed, and watched Esther stand at the sink in the moonlight, her body limned and vivid through the thin cotton night-gown. Hazel felt a flush and a heat. Her eyes shone while she allowed her hunger full rein, devouring the sight yet making no move.

Esther left a few days later. Hazel never considered saying anything to Esther, merely hugging her briefly, feeling the press of her breasts on Esther's as two spots of warmth, as if the sun had joined them momentarily.

Chapter 19

Hazel

The longer I think on it, the more I think this is the only way it could have gone. I spent all my days worrying about Shelly, let alone thinking about taking more waifs in. I found baking for her to do, I found chores for her to do. Why, that 'sell bread to customers' was a thing I thought up right then and there, cuz she looked so lost and hopeless. Even though I'd heard, out at the spring, that a young woman would be coming who needed a shoulder, I had no idea that Shelly would need so much effort from me. Or that I would have to be so sneaky to keep her on an even keel.

Her pride nearly killed her when that idiot customer blurted out how exciting it was to have bread to buy finally. I had to tell her he was a drunk who never remembered that he went back and forth twice a month on his sales route.

I did bake bread that way before the gas stove. A little white lie about selling it? Worth it to save that poor girl from herself.

Chapter 20

Travis

I tell you what, I ain't never worked so hard as those first few days when that little gal Shelly showed up on our porch, carryin' nothin but a sad face. Confuses the heck outta me cuz Hazel is always talkin' about how she 'hears' that she is supposed to care for all kinds a people. Well, there ya go, one just sittin' there for the helpin', and it was like Hazel wanted to take her back to the return counter and see if they had a different model.

You don't get to pick what stuff makes you take a stand. You stand there and defend whatever you got lookin' for protection behind you. All there is to it.

It took me a good while to make those two girls like each other, that's for sure.

Chapter 21

New Family

Back before Opal and Claire, Hazel and Shelly would make a roast—pork, on rare occasions, and beef more commonly—or a roaster full of chicken accompanied with baked potatoes, churned butter, carrots, and some type of beans. After Shelly showed up, she started to expand the table with fresh bread. Mashed potatoes took the place of baked potatoes. Green beans with thick cuts of bacon showed up about this time, too. Opal and Claire didn't know a table; the eating Opal had done back in Taos, more like subsistence foraging, didn't count. In any case, these meals were way different than what Opal had ever seen.

Truth be told, Opal ate to bursting those days—enjoying the company of the older Shelly, and the usually untethered stories that Travis often started and then forgot to finish. Baby Claire ate green bean after green bean, mashing them in her mouth and allowing the puree to drip out both sides of her mouth when she grinned at them.

Opal, five years later, released from whatever trouble she'd lived under, now flourished and thrived out in the simple desert. Her straight black hair shone in both sun and moonlight. She wanted no part of the cold water wash at the pump routine; she reveled in a hot bath at night while Hazel and Shelly spoiled little Claire. Her breasts, smallish until Claire was born, filled her bra now. She had muscular legs that often strained the fabric of her khaki pants. She had some skirts and two dresses, but she preferred to wear pants when she went out to take care of the stock. It wouldn't do to trip over folds of skirt while a pack of hungry hogs raced her to the feeding trough. Her arms were wiry and tan; she carried buckets of feed, buckets of milk, and threw bales of hay around without a thought. Farmers and ranchers were the first fitness buffs, after all.

"Get off my damned foot, you big old cow," Opal shouted.

The cow turned to look at her, lazily chewed her cud, and stepped away.

"What the heck? Is this the first time you've done this?" she said, still to the placid milk cow.

Opal hopped around for a second, but knew the damage was mild, and the infraction was inadvertent. Opal ended up chuckling and rubbing the cow's head, leaning down to milk her of that fine, fresh, frothy milk.

"You don't mean anything by it, do ya?" she laughed.

The cow burped up a glob of grass and chewed, contented.

Opal pulled the milk from the udder and thought about what it meant to stay here these years, trying to be obedient to the pull that Claire felt, clumsy as Claire was at telling her they were supposed to stay here.

She thought back to the first time Claire had said something.

"Mama? Do you hear that?" she'd said.

"I don't know what you mean," Opal said.

"That voice always says stuff when we walk by that wall."

"What old wall?"

"The one. Right back there. It used to be a house. Hazel and Travis used to live there."

"Who told you that? And how can that be? There's nothing there," Opal countered.

"Well, there is a wall, anyway. The voice tells me it used to be a house. Way back when. I always get sad when we go by there, though."

"You'll have to show me when we go back, ok? Why do you get sad?"

"You don't hear it? It says you do," Claire said doubt-fully.

"I certainly did not. But I was thinking. Maybe I missed it."

"Yeah, that's probably it. Can we go to the spring? I want to see it, too," Claire said.

"I think that's a great idea! Want to go there first or the ravine first?" Opal asked.

"Oh, let's go to the ravine. Then we can sit by the spring and dip our feet in, ok?"

"Deal."

Opal and Claire had done just that, and Opal was shocked to realize it was only a year or two ago that Claire had begun to exhibit this 'talk with the land' tendency. It alarmed her, sure. As a mother, especially, but as a plain human, too. She hadn't come from a place where 'talking to the land' was done, or accepted, or cherished, or pursued. And she'd be damned before she went to a phone and called back to Claire's father to ask if his family had that kind of voodoo relationship with 'the land'. Spooky.

"On balance, though, maybe it's genetic, rather than psychotic. Not sure which I pick," Opal muttered.

Then she finished the milking, cleaned the equipment, released the cows back into the pasture, and carried the milk back inside.

Chapter 22

Opal

"I'm so glad I finally found you again," she murmured.

He hugged her tightly to him, squeezing the space and distance that had come between them. She felt the closeness. The long-present anxiety dissipated from her conscious thought, calm as a benevolent flood. Like when the Nile used to flood, and the people of the valley blessed the mud that would soon turn to fertile soil. The few people that drowned, acceptable losses.

"You know I didn't mean to hurt you. It's just that you get me mad when you argue with me," her boyfriend said in the dream.

"Just because I don't agree, doesn't mean I want to leave," she murmured.

"I'm runnin' things, you gotta get that straight."

"Still, I don't think we should be using this stuff anymore. We've got a baby to think of now."

"I'll stop when I'm good and ready. You can sit and watch me or join on in," he said.

Opal held the brand-new baby in her arms, looked into those flawless brown eyes that held only trust and no pain. She looked up at her boyfriend, Davis, whose name she didn't say out loud when she was awake, and saw in his eyes all the pain that was missing from her baby's eyes. All the anger that Opal held at him, she hid from her own eyes—lest he get even angrier.

"I already told the agency that we'd be bringing them a baby today. My decision's final," he said.

"You maybe oughta asked me what I thought about that first," Opal said, stepping away from him.

"Give me the baby. I'll take it myself."

In the dream, she turned to run, tripped over the mattress on the floor, turned while falling to protect her baby. The baby squalled. The boyfriend stretched and grabbed for first the baby, then Opal's hair, then Opal's neck. She started choking and her vision grayed. The baby screamed its first humiliation and pain.

Opal woke in a flush, looking wildly around the room for the boyfriend. Not seeing him, she reached for her baby, remembering as she woke that she had named her Claire. That it had been five years since she left. A deep, shuddering breath brought her back to the bedroom of Gladstone

House. Safe. No more hitting. Not found. Not adopted. Safe.

"You ok, Mama?" Claire asked.

"Oh, honey. I think so. I just had a bad dream, is all."

"You need to go see them. You need to find out more about why he was always so mad at you," Claire said quietly, her head on the pillow next to Opal.

"I always am surprised you know what I dreamed about, sweetie."

"Do you know how to find them? Back there?"

"I doubt it. I guess I could go back to the house. See who is still there," she said. "Why would I, though?"

"You need to tell him about me. He needs to know what Gladstone tells me."

"There's no way that Hazel, Travis, or Shelly want any part of that man on this property. It doesn't matter that you're his child."

"The sod house. He's supposed to come and sit inside the sod house."

Opal was suddenly weary. Wearier than when they had gone to bed last night. Faced with the grim history of a male who spawned her child, and the possibility that he deserved a spot here, in her haven, soaked her nerves with a spanging tension. Like a hinge that opens part way, stops, and the person knows that forcing the hinge fully open will cause the mechanism to fail and the door to swing crookedly, dangerously, uselessly. Her flight from Taos, infant clutched to her stomach, towards safety in the distance, threatened by this pronouncement from a precocious five-year-old.

"No."

"It's the wrong thing to tell me 'no', Mama," Claire said.

"You may be special, but you are *not* in charge. I say no."

"You'll be sorry," Claire said, as she bounced off the edge of the bed to her feet. Her long blonde hair swung freely, a few strands flying up wildly, and another patch stuck to her face and forehead from the combination of sleep spit and pillow where she'd lain.

"I'm already sorry, Claire. There's no reason to talk about how we left, or who we left, or why. You don't need to know the details; just know you don't have a father," Opal said. Softly, the bitterness buried still.

Hazel stuck her head in the bedroom.

"You girls want some breakfast? I've got beef sausage, eggs, and pancakes almost ready. Oh, I see little Claire has already gotten up! Opal, want to join us?" she said cheerily.

"I'm starved!" proclaimed Claire, skipping out of the bedroom with Hazel. She turned back to her mother.

"I *do* have a father. I want to meet him."

Opal sank back into the pillow, saying, "I'll be out in a second, Hazel. Thank you."

Chapter 23

Claire

I don't think it matters. But I know I am supposed to want to take care of everybody. I don't mean like feed them and do all the work—I'm only a kid. I mean, I am supposed to make sure they are safe from the bad voice. And that they listen to the good voice. My mother says I should do what I know is right, even if it isn't fun.

Well, this isn't fun. But it's the only way I can save Shelly from hating herself, Hazel from thinking she wasted her whole life, Travis from, well, losing his mind all the way, and Mom from always being afraid of whoever my dad is in Taos. Or wherever we ran from when I was a little baby.

And so what if I can read people's minds or see into their heads? I don't think of it like that, anyway. I just can tell what is going on in them. It's mostly pictures, but some-times, if I know the words, I'd be able to explain it to them so they can understand. My mother gets it, because I've been doing it ever since I could talk. Well, I could do it before I could talk, but she didn't realize that. It just took me learning to talk for Mom to see I was different. Different in a safer way, not a creepy way. Shelly thinks I'm creepy,

I can tell. I know her dad kicked her out of the house when she was my mom's age, but I'm not sure why. Knowing her, she'll probably tell me. I'll make sure she has a chance to tell me; it's always easier that way if I get it all set up.

Hazel—now there's an old woman who needs some help. She's lived her whole life out here, and has hardly been anywhere else. She hears the voices as clearly as I do, but she doesn't believe she's done the right thing about them. I can tell. She mopes around all day except she pretends not to mope around and fakes like she is serious and holy and a helper. Which she's pretty good at, but I wish she was at least honest about why. She's going to die soon. I need to find a way to tell Mom so she isn't freaked out. Mom and I will be the only two left here by the time Hazel dies.

Travis, you say? Yeah, his mind is mostly toasted. He can't help it; he just got old. I know he did something horrible a long time ago. I need to get him to tell us about that before he stops rocking in his rocker.

Anyway, I'm the one that the good voice, out by the spring, has asked to take care of Gladstone Property, these four people who live here now, and the at-least-two-more people who will be coming soon who need a place.

Mama hears those voices, too. She is scared of them. And that's why she tells me she doesn't hear them. I know.

I don't have to be the new person until Hazel dies. But I can't tell how far away that is. The spring won't tell me. Maybe it doesn't know, but it probably does. Then there's going to be new people who come, and those are the ones I need to look after. Plus, my father.

All I'm supposed to do now is get him to come to Gladstone.

Chapter 24

Travis and Opal

Opal and Claire had been on their way back out to explore some more around the original homestead. Shelly, Hazel, and Opal had discussed it that morning at the breakfast table.

"So—what's the deal with that original square sod house or adobe house or whatever?" Opal asked. Shelly and Hazel both sat at the table with her, and Claire sat in the old wooden high chair, scrabbling bits of biscuit back and forth across the surface.

"Oh my. That's the original house, Opal. When I think of my parents, all of my memories are of us living in that dark little place," Hazel said somberly.

"It was? I can't imagine actually having that as the *only* place to live in!" Opal marveled.

"I've always kind of wondered where that original house was; it's weird that you found it before I cared enough to look for it," Shelly said.

"Well, to be fair, Shelly, you've never looked very far for anything to do," Hazel said with a wry grin.

"Touché. I hope you're convinced by now that I really don't want anything to do with the rest of the world, girls," Shelly said with a laugh.

"I get that about you, Shelly. I mean, I don't *get it*, but I get it, ya know?" Opal said.

They chuckled, and rose without further conversation other than to help each other clear the table, wash the few dishes and pots they cooked in, and then wandered off to their own set of tasks for the day. Opal slung Claire on her hip and headed up the road.

"I'll go check on Travis."

Travis thought back to the day when he realized he was in charge. James and Lily had talked about leaving, and Travis was the only sane adult left on the property. Nathan acted sane, sure, but Travis knew good and well that Nathan had already curdled.

Travis sat in the sun, his face warmed, and replayed the conversation with his older brother.

"Nathan, what the hell are we going to do now?"

"I'll thank you not to curse. The Lord will turn His back on those who curse Him," Nathan said severely.

"I didn't take anyone's name in vain. And what are we going to *do?*" Travis said weakly.

"The Lord Almighty will lead us out of this wilderness, and—"

"Oh, stop. I mean what are we going to do? What are we going to do for money? What are we going to do to keep the livestock alive? How will we get to and from town?"

Nathan took a big breath of air, ready to intone, but Travis forestalled him with first a hand in his face, then by dropping his arm along Nathan's shoulders.

"Look. I know you are just as scared in there as I am. I know you can't admit it. *No*, I get it. You—"

"I'll have you know that I feel no fear. Yea, tho I walk through the Valley of Death, I will fear no Evil," Nathan countered, his voice quavering.

"Yes. I know that verse as well as you do, brother," he pulled him into a full-on hug, rare for these two.

"I made a mistake," Nathan whispered before sobbing.

"What?"

Nathan sobbed on Travis's fresh linen shirt. Travis leaned his head on his younger, shorter brother's head, and tears dripped down the side of his face through the spindly beard. Travis was 16 and Nathan was 15. Hazel was eight. And they were all alone against the traveling world that passed by their property every few days. It got so Travis decided he had imagined Nathan saying he'd made a mistake. He didn't pursue it with Nathan. He didn't forget it, though. That comment sat there, right over his left shoulder, always murmuring just below audible.

Travis didn't even know who he was supposed to tell that James and Lily were dead. He was pretty sure it was ok to bury them, so he did that. Travis beseeched small Hazel into writing each parent's name on the horizontal piece of wood. Then they hammered the crosses at the head of each grave. Hazel picked a few sprigs of sage, bundled them together with twine, and then threaded a few cholla blooms along each bundle. She laid the bundles at the foot of the crosses. After a few weeks, and a brief rain shower or two, the ground had sunk so Travis went back and laid another layer of the sandy dirt atop the graves. It was too depressing to see actual depressions in the ground to mark them. At least if there was a small rise one could fool oneself into thinking that there was still some hope for them all.

Back in the present, Travis wished there had been a different way. But as with most waking nightmares, it always ended with the three deaths that changed Hazel forever. Changed them both forever.

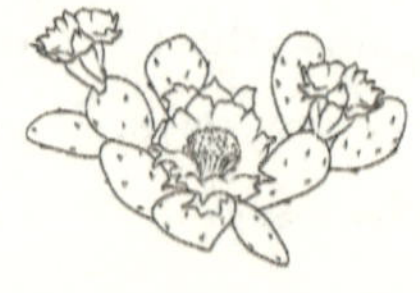

Chapter 25

Travis and Opal

Travis, thinking back to the feel of the spade in his hands, rubbed his arthritic, still-gnarled hands together while he sat on the porch. He knew that the three of them had survived the loss of James and Lily, but even on his good days didn't remember the day in and day out struggles, triumphs, and failures that comprised their lives those years.

"We didn't have any choice back then, did we, Nathan?" he asked.

As he spoke, Opal rounded the corner of his cabin and heard him speak.

"What's that, Travis?"

"I said, we didn't have any choice back then, did we, Hazel?" he said, looking at Opal.

Opal smiled nervously, then said, "We sure didn't. Do you remember what the hardest thing was?" she said, after a pause.

"Oh, boy," Travis ran his hand along his whiskered jaw, dislodging a remnant of scrambled eggs in the process. "I guess I'd have to say the toughest thing was talking Hazel out of always trying to run off and find her parents."

"She tried to run off? Where'd she think they were?"

Opal settled Claire on the porch, handing her a wooden spoon and trowel from the garden for her to play with. Claire gurgled happily and gently banged the spoon on Opal's leg. Claire crawled closer to Travis and started tapping Travis's leg with the trowel.

"Well, I guess she must've thought her parents had gone into town. They went a few times a year. Hell, they probably went once a month back when Hazel was little. Before we got out here, anyway. Once me and Nathan got here they usually sent us. We always had a rowdy streak, and somehow wandering along the street in Springer shook that out of us."

Opal didn't remark on how Travis had somehow lumped her, Claire, and Hazel all into one female character that threaded through his short story of the time after James and Lily's death. She'd tried a few times before to diagram for him who was whom, and what year it was, and why she wasn't an actual relative, but it never stuck. Travis was so damned good-natured about it that it somehow felt churlish to keep telling him what he was confused about.

"She sure does like to bang on things, don't she?" Travis chuckled as he leaned forward in his rocker and watched Claire hit him with the trowel.

"Yeah, she'll do that all day if you let her," Opal agreed.

"She did the same thing with that old milk bottle and stick back when her mother and father died. Nathan and I had no earthly idea how to get her to stop it, either," he said. "Nathan and I were hopeless in the kitchen. She knew how to cook and even to bake, and we could barely get her to stop wool-gathering long enough to cook dinner. Hell, any meal at all, really. She'd just sit and sniffle, and then take to clinking that same bottle. Over and over. You remember that, Nathan?" Travis turned to look behind him.

"She must've come out of it ok, right? How long did it take?" Opal asked him, laying a hand on his forearm.

"Well, and this is funny. I remember this like it was yesterday," he grinned.

It was as if a switch had flipped. His chin drooped to his chest, his eyes fluttered a few times, and then fully closed.

"Welp, I guess we will have to wait until next time to hear the rest of the story, right, Claire?" Opal said and smiled, scooping the baby up and stepping quietly off the porch.

Opal's curiosity was piqued, though. What did old Travis remember so well it felt like yesterday? She arranged to have Hazel and Shelly keep an eye on Claire the next morning.

Which was no big deal, really. Opal was her mother, but she was being raised by all three women with very little regard for boundaries. Claire was a happy young child and needed little discipline. The example she saw of all three of them working and then eating together with Travis gave Claire few chances to show discontent. She didn't know anything else.

Opal walked over to Travis's cabin in the morning sun, a brisk fall day with the smell of frost moving past her in the breeze off the mountains in the distance. He wasn't on the front porch, or the back porch either after she rounded the corner. She knocked once on the wooden screen door, but barely paused as she moved inside. The wood stove was ticking, either from being warmed up or from cooling down. He got up so early it could be either one. The milk cows produced best if he got the morning milking done around five, so he could've been out and back already. On the other hand, the hogs didn't like to rouse themselves to eat until they could feel the sun on the building after a solid sunrise. She rarely thought of it, but now realized that, if she wanted to know more of the story of the property, she'd better pay attention to the rhythms that Travis followed.

As she sat at his kitchen table in one of the two chairs, he came around the corner from the bedroom, buckling his belt and straightening his tucked shirt.

"Well, hello, there, Opal. What brings you in today?"

"Hi, uh, Travis. Oh, nothing, I was just bored and wondered what you were up to," she said.

"I've seen to the milking, but I was just on my way back out to slop the hogs. Want to come along?"

"Absolutely I do. As long as I don't have to get too muddy!" she laughed.

"Pigs? Muddy? I don't think that's a thing, young lady," he laughed right with her.

Chapter 26

Travis and Opal

He held the door for her, ushered her through with his free arm, and then snagged a cap from the Clayton Co-op off the peg by the door to settle on his head before he followed her out the door. They strode off towards the south along the ranch road. He took the left rut, and she took the right one once they passed the barn and the road devolved into the two ruts that led out and past the adobe buildings. The first one they came to held the pigs. Before she stepped to the door, she turned to Travis.

"You said the other day that you remembered something about when Hazel finally quit mourning her parents. Like it was yesterday, you said. Do you remember having that conversation?"

"Hmm. Did I? I'm sorry to say I don't remember that conversation. But that doesn't mean I don't remember what she did to quit mourning poor James and Lily. I certainly do remember that."

"What did she do?"

"It wasn't what she did. It was what she quit doing that I remember so well."

Opal, treading lightly, merely said, "Oh?"

"We've got time for a story, right? I can talk while we check the pigs."

"Sure, Travis. What can I do to help?"

"Nah, nothin'. I've got it. It's a whole routine which I remember better if I just do it all start to finish. Here— just perch on that chest right there. I won't need to get into it, at least I don't think I will."

Opal settled herself on the heavy wooden chest, which looked like it used to be some other piece of furniture maybe.

"Yeah. That used to be a big old piano. Someone from Illinois had dragged it all this way in their wagon. Spoiled wife or daughter, I bet. Anyway, one of their oxen died back a few days and they finally listened to reason and lightened their load," Travis chuckled. "Now. Where was I?"

"What did Hazel stop doing, is where we were."

"Hazel, poor sweet little orphaned Hazel, eight innocent years old, used to love to eat pork. Day in and day out, all three meals. If she could have pork each one, she'd be ecstatic. In hog heaven, ya might say," Travis laughed out loud at that, looking at Opal to see if she got the joke.

Opal smiled obediently, but didn't laugh; she merely waited for him to continue.

"Well, she didn't even like to cook pork anymore, she told us. She *would* cook it, but she always had such a sour look on her face when she did it, that I hated to ask her to do it more than now and then."

"That must've been a change for you? What did you eat instead?"

"That's just it. How many times can you cook chicken and how many different ways are there? Fried. That's one. Baked, which is horrible. That's two. And I guess you could say chicken and noodles, or chicken and dumplings, or soup. That's three," he finished. "We didn't like that at all—no, sir, we did not."

At this, Opal laughed and said, "Ok, let me get this straight. You, a perfectly grown and independent man, let an eight-year-old make a drastic change to the menu just because she pouted when she cooked? Is that about right?"

Travis stopped his bent-over feeding and checking, straightened his back, and looked at Opal soberly.

"Truth is, Opal, I thought she was going to kill herself to be with them again. I didn't want that to be the final straw."

Chapter 27

Travis and Opal

At that, he bent back to his task of checking each piglet's limbs, snouts, and ears for health. He mucked through the pen to the far wall where the sow was laying, exhausted from her job as a 'we never close' food conversion factory. Opal's smile had disappeared, but she sat quietly atop the remnant of the musical instrument, wondering about Hazel. She waited with Travis while he finished his task list, then they walked silently, contentedly, back to his house. They stopped at the well so he could wash his boots off and his hands off. He carefully sluiced the great flat piece of limestone that served as a wash pad under the pump's flow.

Opal and Travis had walked to the edge of the porch, right before taking each other's leave, before either of them spoke.

"That's when we bought a few more cows," Travis said.

"What's that?" Opal asked.

"When she quit eating pork. That's when we bought more cows."

"Oh, I see."

"You watch. Shelly does most of the cookin' these days, but you watch. When there's anything pork on the table, Hazel just plain won't take it. She may take a piece, but I'll bet you a dollar she won't eat the whole thing. A bite. Mebbe two."

"Why in the world do you think that helps her?"

"She told us. One day, after we were pretty sure she was done with the suicide thing, at least we weren't so worried about it, we asked her. I said, 'Now, Hazel, I know you don't take to pork no more, but I can't figure out for the life of me why. What's goin' on with that?' I figured she'd blow her top. She didn't."

"What'd she do?"

"She looked me smack in the eye and said, 'That's what Nathan smelled like after he was dead. When he burned. I just can't do it.'"

"Oh, god."

"Yeah. So that shut me up real good. I hugged her. I mean, kinda. I never was much of a hugger," Travis said softly. "And I'll tell you what—she went on to bed and never said another word about it. Still hasn't, as far as I know."

"News to me, that's for sure."

"A course, I don't hear so good so she maybe *is* cussing me out good and proper every day. Haw, haw, haw!" he cackled, slapping his knee.

"Oh, I don't think she does *any* cussing. At least not any that I hear. I don't know that I've ever seen her lose her temper, now that we're talking about it," Opal remarked.

"Naw, she's pretty steady, ain't she? Welp, I'll say goodnight to ya. I enjoyed your help and company today. Say goodnight to the other three for me, will ya?"

"Of course, Travis. And thank *you* for letting me slow you down with your chores," she said, smiling at him.

A cloud crossed the sun briefly, and brought that tiny shiver of chill that came to every desert when the sun subtracted itself.

Chapter 28

Shelly and Hazel

After Opal had turned the corner of the cabin on her way to see Travis, Shelly turned to Hazel.

"So, do you miss them?"

"Who? My parents?"

"Yeah. I mean, it's been so long, I just wondered if—"

"Oh, gosh. I feel this split personality inside me. I'm this grown old woman and I've lived all these days. And yet, when a splash of melancholy hits me, I'm a little kid again and I'm burying my face in my mother's skirt or my father's sheepskin coat."

"I don't remember ever hugging my father," Shelly said.

"Oh, gosh, I hugged my father all the time. He was so good-natured about it. Not like a lot of fathers way back then. Spare the rod, spoil the child, was pretty much the entire child-raising advice back then."

"My father certainly knew that one," Shelly said with some bitterness.

"No, my father never raised a hand to me, Shell," Hazel said. "Of course, I was pretty compliant. I mean, what else was there to do out here? We went to town, but mother didn't let go of my hand at all until she handed me back up into the wagon when we headed home," Hazel said.

"Was there anything for you to do in town when you got there?" Shelly asked. "Not like there was a playground or an amusement park back then, right?"

"As if. No, Mama usually let me carry some of the dry goods we bought from the general store. I still remember how that brown paper rattled when they wrapped up the cloth or the flour we bought. Only one hand's worth, though, because she always wanted me to keep one hand free to hang on to hers."

"Sounds like heaven. If my father had a free hand, he was just as likely to slap me as he preached a verse to me. 'For my own good,' he'd always say. As if that excused him," Shelly said. "But that was another time. It isn't now. And I'm glad of it," she finished.

"Sounds like your father was stuck further back in time than my father was," Hazel remarked.

"My father did love those Calvinists and their pessimism. When was that popular?"

They both laughed, rubbed each other's shoulders, and moved to the next thing on the day's list. They'd lived together for so many years that these conversations took place with no fanfare.

Chapter 29

Opal

As Opal walked the property more extensively, she discovered, way back towards the edge, two partial walls of adobe. Not in use. Not usable. But unmistakably a structure that *had* been in use in the not-too-distant past.

She knew from her time in the Taos valley that adobe stood for hundreds of years, especially if it was maintained. Adobe that had been left to the elements in many cases still stood; it had just been subsumed by dust and sand and debris, carried on winds from every direction. Since she could see two walls that rose only to waist height, she took several steps back to see what the general shape of the land was. The land sloped gently, almost imperceptibly, towards the Rockies still almost 100 miles west, but the area immediately around the two walls looked much like an anthill did out in the scrub. A clear spot, at least formerly cleared, that had a mound in the middle. A puzzle. One that she thought might be a diversion for her, and a shovel, one afternoon after the temperatures cooled enough to avoid heatstroke.

Several months later, then, with Claire along in first a baby backpack, then left to play in the cleared spot of dirt around the walls, Opal slid the straight shovel down the edge of the adobe, pulling gently toward her in an effort to separate the loose, sandy dirt from the original structure. This technique seemed to produce results and avoided damaging the original mud, which, if it turned out to be an artifact of some tribe or other, or even a structure associated with an offshoot of the Pony Express, would be important. She doubted that it would be worth much in any historical sense, but it didn't hurt to be careful, and besides, her curiosity was sparked by the 'why' of it. The Gladstone House was out of sight from this far south. Claire gurgled happily while scritching one hand in the dirt, and the other hand swinging a small stick of mesquite that Opal had handed her.

The wall cleared easily down two or three feet, which made the wall, if it had stood on leveled ground, high enough for a cabin. Of course there would have been no plumbing or electricity to this distant spot, but most old structures didn't have this anyway, so it was unremarkable. Neither of the two walls had any openings, though, and Opal wondered at the possibility of claustrophobia in that. She followed one wall around the corner to where there was barely a rise of any remnant of wall. She scuffed the shovel along a line where she thought a wall would run, but found nothing. It had been a diverting afternoon, but she had other work to do, so she strapped Claire back on her back, and headed for the livestock.

She brought it up at supper. "Do you two know anything about that fallen-down adobe way back along the road?" she asked.

"There's a building out there?" Shelly asked.

"Oh, heck yeah, I remember that building! James said never to go in there!" Travis crowed.

He'd been eating steadily and, at his advanced age, often forgot to chew and swallow before he began speaking. A thin line of diluted mashed potatoes leaked out of one corner of his mouth.

"Now, Travis, there's no way you could remember anything way out there," Hazel cautioned.

Hazel's eyes had taken a cautious cast when she said that, glancing at Travis but then holding Opal's gaze right after.

"Why were you out there, Opal?"

"Oh, no reason really. I wanted to see if I could find an antelope or a few to show to Claire," she said.

Claire showed much the same gusto for the mashed potatoes as Travis did, but showed no interest at all in her mama talking about any animals to look for out on the high steppe.

"Well, I guess I've not ventured that far out there, at least not enough to remember seeing anything," Hazel said.

"I walked out there once when I got here. That would've been 20 years ago, at least," Shelly said. "I didn't see a damned thing that interested me, and my reason for going out there was one I hate to think on."

"Oh? Why'd you go out there?" Opal asked.

"Remember what your answer is to us whenever we ask about Taos?"

"Uh, yeah. I don't like to talk about that."

"Same here," Shelly said firmly, but with a gentle smile and a hand on Opal's arm.

"Some stuff we just don't bring up. It's just easier," Hazel agreed.

The conversation stuck with Opal next time she wandered out to the old adobe ruin with the shovel. She scuffed a line along one probable wall, then joined the fourth side with more scuffing. It wasn't a huge structure, not even ten feet square, but there was still a lot of dirt that needed moving for her to find the third and fourth wall foundations. They were there, all right. Just one course of adobe that sat above the packed ground. She continued to dig until she felt like she'd found the original floor and had excavated the interior down to right angles at the base.

"Why in the world would they build an outbuilding this far out?" she wondered.

Chapter 30

The Assessor

"So, you want to do *what* again? Make a campground out of this place?" the assessor asked.

"Well, not exactly, sir. We just want to run some more power cables out to a few concrete pads, maybe a half-dozen, so in the case of a tired RV full of campers who want to quit driving, they could just park here," Shelly replied.

"Well, how the hell are you gonna come up with the power for all this? The wires are all on the far side of the highway, and this one strand you've had since way before the code changed won't carry any more power than it already does. County won't allow it, anyway," he said.

He'd been on the property less than ten minutes, standing on the porch for less than five, and Hazel had already gotten angry enough to go back into the kitchen to get something, saying she'd be right back. Clearly, he was an officious hack who wasn't used to driving this far from his county office with the squeaking office chair and his solitaire game on the county's dime.

"We don't need you to solve all of *that* for us, Mr. Glen," Opal said. "We just need to get preliminary approval to start taking bids for all the work that we'd have to do."

"Well, that makes sense. But, mark my words, this'll cost you way more than you think it will, and it'll take you about double the time you think it will," he said severely.

"There is no possible way that you have any idea how long or how expensive we already think all this is going to be," Hazel said through the screen door, walking back into the conversation by parting the pink gingham curtain between the kitchen and the sales counter.

"We don't need your pessimistic attitude poisoning our plan. And if we've had our few doubts, we darned sure wouldn't share them with you. You and your darned county seat government are part of the problem," she said.

"Hazel—take it easy. He's just doing his job," Shelly said calmly.

"Now, Miss Gladstone, that's right. I'm just doing my job. I'm not trying to pour water on your campfire," Mr. Glen quickly agreed.

"May I suggest you open that snappy little metal pad and start filling out papers, then? And do indeed leave the worrying to us, why don't you?" Hazel said.

"Of course, ma'am. That's my job," he said with a cha-grined bow. "Ok. Let me get some measurements and some estimates. Who's the best person to work with on all of that?"

"I'm the inside gal," Shelly said. "And Opal's the outside gal. We can take turns telling you what you need. Is it alright if we both just follow you around? Try to get underfoot and slow you down?" Shelly smiled at him to show that all was forgiven.

"That'd be great. It'll work out much easier if I get it right the first time," he said.

"Now, Mr. Glen, so there's no hard feelings, why don't you come sit down in the kitchen for a second and have a glass of tea," Hazel offered.

"Well, now I—"

"Nope. You come on back here. Have some tea," Hazel said mildly, while motioning towards her by turning her hand in a circle.

The visit went fine after that—at least until Mr. Glen, while standing with Shelly and Opal in the back farmyard—asked about the cabin and other buildings.

"You got anyone in that there shotgun cabin?" he asked.

"Shotgun cabin? What do you mean by that?" Opal asked him back.

"Well, it's cuz when they built 'em, they say you coulda shot all the way front to back and hit every room. It don't mean nothin' bad, it's just what they used to call the construction."

"Oh. I had heard that a while ago, but didn't really know what it meant," she said. "Uncle Travis lives in there. Does it matter?"

"I don't think so. I just already said there were four residents of Gladstone. I'll need to change that to five. Or is there more?"

"Nope. And, I getcha. Five is all of us," Shelly said cheerily.

They walked the road to the barn, and he peeked his head inside. Satisfied, he stepped right back out onto the road, and nodded his head towards the two adobe buildings down the track.

"Is that one or two old buildings back there? Do I need to go look at them? Are you planning to use them for the RV project?" he asked.

"Oh, no. The one is just livestock. And that farther one is almost a historic place. First building on the land," Opal said. "I take care of most of the stock, although Travis still helps a little."

"Historic place, you say? Was it around when the Santa Fe Trail came by?"

"Oh, yeah, that's almost certain. Travis and Hazel said that was the first house that James Gladstone built to live in and to protect the spring. He had quite a setup helping out the wagons who stopped for either water or repairs."

"Hmm, that may change things. You can't just make a commercial property out of somewhere that used to be part of United States history."

Chapter 31

The Assessor

Opal and Shelly looked at each other, alarmed. Mr. Glen didn't notice because he was still looking off into the distance, shading his eyes with his hand and balancing his clipboard with the other.

"Well, ok, wait. I mean, as far as importance goes, I don't think that adobe hut was actually a very big deal. But—" Opal stopped.

"What she means is that we were going to kind of 'play up' the importance of that hut when people stopped so they'd maybe buy a few more things or stay a night," Shelly added. "Not lie to them. Not at all. But maybe stretch a rumor into an almost-certainty, if you know what I mean."

"Ah. Yeah, I get that. Of course, I'm not the county office that determines the degree of historical nature of a place. You probably ought to write them a letter, too. Make sure they at least get a notice of the project," he said.

"Are you sure that's necessary?" Shelly asked.

"It is. But—" He paused and looked at them both. "I've taken to your vision of this project, so I want to see it succeed. A word of advice to get past the history buffs, if you don't mind me injecting my opinion?"

"Not at all. Please. What say you?"

"I would keep your letter *very* brief. I would not refer specifically to *any* buildings. I would just say 'the Gladstone property' and indicate that you want to run a little bit more electricity and have a few, and this is important, a few *separated* spots of concrete poured for parking. Parking. You don't need to mention camping or RVs or sales or profits or old adobe or wherever that old track goes to when it gets past the adobe. That'll just cause them to send someone out here."

"Ok, that's good advice. We'll remember that."

"Those people in that office are jerks. They think they own everything and can ban everyone from doing anything with anything. The more you can keep them out of your hair, the better, ok?" Mr. Glen said this ruefully, as if he knew that sometimes government was part of the problem.

"Absolutely ok. Thanks," Opal said, patting his upper arm briefly.

His assessment concluded, they walked him out to his government vehicle and watched him toss his notepad carelessly in the passenger seat. He looked up at them from between the door and frame of the car, smiled at them, and sketched a wave.

"Be sure to tell Hazel thanks for the time. And… don't worry about it. Turns out this is a standard assessment—there shouldn't be any hiccups for you," he said lightly.

"Thanks very much. You have a good day now, and drive safe," Shelly hollered.

One more wave and he drove off, eastbound towards Clayton and his office chair.

The women trailed each other up the front steps, through the sales room, and into the kitchen. As expected, they found Hazel sitting at the table with a cup of tea in front of her. Opal hitched Claire on her hip and got tea mugs down from the cupboard with her free hand.

"Tea, Shelly?"

"Sure. Thank you."

They felt collectively wrung out, for some reason. Shelly sat in her chair, her legs splayed out in front of her, one on each side of a table leg.

"This is the first time I think I may be too old for this," Hazel finally admitted, breathing out heavily.

"That guy—he bugs me. There's something about how he looked out there at the old buildings…" Shelly said.

"It's fine. It'll be fine. He's an old, fat, out-of-shape, government lump. That's all it was," Opal said.

"I wish I felt that."

"He wrote a *lot* down when we were standing there talking about the old adobe."

"What did you tell him about the old places?" Hazel said with alarm.

"Yeah, well, get this. Shelly started to say that the old adobe house was from forever ago and that your dad used it to take care of people on the Santa Fe Trail!"

"I had no idea he would give a crap about that, though!" Shelly urged.

"Still. He got all glinty about it. I could tell he had a ton of questions that were about to start bubbling over, so I made up some garbage about us spinning a bunch of stories to drum up business," Opal pressed.

"Did you let him go see it?" Hazel worried.

"Oh, no. Not even close. We barely got past Travis's cabin and we had just stopped in the road. He looked that way, is all," Opal reassured her.

"Because it just won't do for them to go looking too closely at all that out there," Hazel said.

"It's just an old house, right?" asked Opal.

"It *is* just an old house, right, Hazel?" pushed Shelly.

Hazel answered neither of them, lost in thought, with a deep, ancient frown on her face.

"I'm going to go talk to Travis. You two stay here and relax for a few minutes," Hazel finally said. She left the room before either of the other two could even get out of their chairs.

"What the heck was that all about?"

"Beats me. But if I didn't know any better, it sounds like there's more to the origin story than either of us knows," Shelly answered.

"Yeah."

A pause, then Opal shifted in her chair to look at Shelly.

"Did you ever really ask them for details? I mean, when you showed up that first time?"

"Do you mean, did I interview them to see if they were suitable to take in a penniless and pregnant girl from the Ozarks? No, ma'am, I did not."

"Well, I see what you mean. But, surely, after you decided to stay? You had a conversation or two, no?"

Shelly sat and spun her tea cup slowly. "Not really. Listen, you may not have figured this out, but I was a true little mess. Selfish. Self-absorbed. Tragic hero of my own fairy tale. Martyred from my family and from a faith that had no mercy."

"Oh, man, I—"

"No, it's ok. Let me finish. When I got here, Lord, so long ago… I could barely ask for a place to stay. And when Hazel was so kind, and accepting, and, just, so warm. I didn't dare jinx that by wondering what their whole story was. Travis has always been a perfect gentleman. And that's coming from a girl—I used to be a girl, you know—that didn't trust her idiot boyfriend or her granite-faced father."

"Now that I think about it, I never really asked for any history or old stories or anything when we got here, either. I have in the last few days, I guess. Travis has been telling me about what Hazel did after her parents died."

"That's further along than I've ever gotten, I guess. She never says anything about it," Shelly admitted.

"Same here. She'll be sitting there, all sunny, holding Claire, and then will just stare off out the window, the saddest serenity on her face that I've ever seen," Opal related. "Then, her jaw will set, her eyes will just plain shut down. She'll hand me the baby and walk away without a word."

"I've seen her do that, too. Not with the baby, but the quick change," Shelly said.

"I just put it down to her never living anywhere else or regrets about never finding a husband or having kids of her own. I don't know; maybe it's not that simple."

They sat at the table for another few minutes. Shelly pushed herself up then and started working on food preparations for supper. Opal said she and Claire were going to go out and check on the animals. A small smile passed between them as a promise to meet back in the kitchen for supper.

Chapter 32

The Assessor

Meanwhile, Hazel had stepped on the porch of the shotgun cabin that Travis lived in and slung the screen door wide open to enter. She didn't bother to knock. She stepped quickly through his kitchen, which was dusty and hardly used, and traveled deeper to find him in his small living room. No lights were on, which made the room gloomy and full of shadows, even on what was a sunny day outside.

He sat in his one plush chair. His tall, thin, increasingly frail body sat enveloped in the cushion of the brocade fabric, each arm strung out along the armrests. His head drooped a little, although his eyes were open and seeking hers as she entered the room. His thin gray hair strung in sparse locks across the top of his head, smoothed in place with his hand and clearly not combed that way. He had on old Wrangler jeans and a cowboy shirt with mother-of-pearl buttons. He had heavy socks on his feet but no shoes or boots.

"Hullo, there, Hazel," he said mildly.

"Uncle. Good afternoon. We may have a problem," she said slowly.

"You aren't talkin' about the livestock, are you?"

"No. I wish."

She stepped across his feet and settled herself in the old, carved walnut chair that sat near him. She perched on the front of the chair rather than pushing all the way back into it. More like a red-tailed hawk on a fence post than a chicken on the roost.

"It's the old house. The adobe one that we started in."

"Uh-huh? What about it?"

"We should have knocked it down better and scattered the blocks better. They found it and want to know about it."

"Who found it? And who wants to know about it?" Travis asked. None of the fog of age showed in his face now; a keen sense of danger sketched his brow. His questions showed a mind trying to assess a danger and how best to combat it.

"It's that damned RV park idea that started it all. I figured it'd keep Opal here, but busy and occupied. So she'd stay *away* from the south of the property. You know, develop the storefront idea and all that, remember?" Hazel said with venom.

"I told you. That's a mistake waiting to happen right there."

"Yes, you did. It's too late now. Pandora is out of the box and floating around this whole place."

"It wasn't Pandora in the box, you know. It was evil. And it *was* locked into the box, where we shoulda kept it," Travis said darkly.

"Anyway. They got an assessor to come out here and make sure we could do the work so it would be legal and we could get a permit. I told them we never had a permit before to sell stuff. They kept saying the world's moved on and you can't just do stuff—you have to get permission. So I relented," Hazel said.

"Shit. So you let them invite an outsider onto Gladstone?" he said incredulously.

"Worse. A government guy. He and his bossy clipboard walked all over like he owned the place and we were begging for food scraps. I about got sick to my stomach watching Shelly and Opal moon all over him," Hazel said disgustedly.

"Shit. Well, what's the damage, then?" Travis finally asked.

"That's just it. It doesn't seem like there *was* any damage. They scared me when they said he asked about the old adobe place, but then they said he didn't need to walk out there and look at it, so I thought we'd dodged a bullet," she said slowly.

"Ok? What's got you all shook then?"

"It's the girls. Now *they* want to know if that's just a plain old house where we all lived or what."

"What the hell did you tell them? Not the truth, I hope," he pleaded.

"Good Lord, no. I didn't answer them. I came straight out here to figure out what we are gonna do."

"I've got a confession, too, then."

"Oh?" she said, arching a brow at him.

"Yeah. You know how Opal always likes to help do the chores. Does a lot of them now, as a matter of fact. I don't get around as quick as I like. Sometimes she's already at it when I get my bones warmed up enough—"

"I know all that. Tell me," she said severely.

"Right. Well, she got to asking me about your mom and pop's deaths. I slipped once and said that you changed your behavior after they died. I hoped she'd move on, and I acted like I'd fallen asleep, so thought I got away with it."

"Oh, crap. She never forgets a tale, does she?"

"Nope. Sure enough not. The next day, she walked out to the pig house with me and asked me about it again."

"What did she ask you?" she said with alarm.

"She said that I said that your behavior changed and it wasn't something you did, but something you stopped doing after they died. So I—"

"Oh, my God. You didn't tell her?"

"No, no. But I had to tell her *something*. So I told her you stopped eating pork. Because you said Nathan smelled like pork after he died. And then we got cows."

"Shit," she said.

They sat in stunned silence as they realized how their carefully spun life and history unraveled at a speed that scared them both.

"All these years. No one knowing," Travis said quietly.

"I should never have let Shelly stay. I should've turned Opal away, too," Hazel admitted.

"Wait a minute. Who knew? We couldn't have known. You can't live like that," he said.

"Well, what if they send out some officer of the law? They'll start asking questions. Three graves instead of two? Where'd you say Nathan went to again? They'll figure it all out, Uncle Travis. All of it!"

"I don't think so. It can't happen. Will anyone care, anyway?"

"We'd better hope not."

Chapter 33

Hazel

Lord, these people. Can't they just let me help them without having a mind of their own? There is no way on God's green earth that an RV park is any kind of an idea. Serves me right for thinking on my own about what would keep Opal here. Claire knows she has to stay. I can see it when she sits on the porch and is just looking out past the spring and the arroyo. I should have trusted Claire to keep Opal here.

Shelly is already gone—her body hasn't caught up to her mind yet. She will leave to go find those horrible parents one day soon. And that'll end in tears. I wish I could tell her.

Chapter 34

The Assessor

Mr. Glen, out of shape though he may be, had an astute mind. And once he got his teeth sunk into a project, he was way more like a bulldog than a terrier. He liked to think that he'd keep hold on a bone like a bulldog that was happy to keep his jaw locked until the other dog just plain suffocated, rather than a terrier who made a huge fuss, nipped a little, and caused hardly any damage. Those women wanted a permit to make some money? He'd be glad to oblige, just as soon as he dug through a dusty room full of county tax records, property deeds, bills of sale, and yes, a visit to the registrar of historic places across the hall. He ate lunch with the guys from that office nearly every day. He'd smelled more than his share of their farts in the conference room after a heavy lunch over at the café. He was entitled to a little of their zeal doing an hour or two of focused research.

"Gladstone, huh? Well, let's just see what you have to tell me," he murmured as he navigated through the county software to see what records they already had on file. He spent a good hour walking through the deeds, files, plats, and tax receipts. Mostly boring, but a few *very* interesting tidbits—or lack of tidbits—that captured his attention.

"Charlie? Yeah, it's Dave over here in the assessor's office. I have a few questions for you when you get a second," he said into the phone. "Well, frankly, it'd be easier if you came over to my office. It's hard to show you what I mean over the phone." A pause. "Sure, I'll be here all afternoon. Come on over and I'll see ya when I see ya."

Charlie, a grizzled veteran of the bureaucratic wars of the great Southwest, stepped into Dave Glen's office a little short of two hours later. It was closing on four o'clock, which was when all long-term, self-respecting rural county workers punched out for the day.

"I thought I'd just step in and see what your main theme was, even if we can't get it all answered today," Charlie said.

"Hey, there, Charlie! I'd about given up on you for the day. Glad to see you," Dave said, extending his hand. They shared a sincere handshake, borne from years of working thankless cases together and separately. Most of the time, the best case that could happen out of their respective offices was that the customer requesting the help didn't write back a nasty note cussing them out for being inept or ruling against them.

"It's Gladstone. Does that name ring a bell?"

"Hmm. Small, unincorporated, highway-side, has some obscure history as a religious colony?"

"I shoulda known you'd know it. Have y'all ever been out there to see if it should be protected?"

"Hmm. That's a good question. We can check right quick. They find something?" Charlie asked.

"No, I don't think so. I think it's more like they want to start making some money. But I'm pretty sure they want to walk people out past some old ruins, and I just got to wondering if we ought to help them preserve whatever they have out there. It's not *that* far from Rabbit Ears and, uh—"

"Capulin. Yeah, you're right. That's old Native stuff. Can I sit? You mind if I log in?" Charlie asked.

"Why don't you take that desk right there? Nadine has already left for the day. Just use her terminal and you can pull up all your stuff so we can compare it to mine," Dave offered.

"Yep. Let's do it."

Chapter 35

Harris Health Spa

When Lily, long before her first baby or the birth of Hazel, first stepped down from the truck's running board, she walked south until she found the arroyo. The tent made of canvas, and the frame, looked as if it had come from another age. The tent marked the spot, right at the head of the ravine, where the spring was. This was the famous spring that the original settler, named Harris, claimed as holy water. Well, the first colonial settler, that is. The Jicarilla Apache, Kiowa, and Comanche all knew it to be a sacred place; the water from the spring important to them for more than just hydration. Harris preached to everyone who pulled up and circled a wagon for the night about the healing properties of the spring, and "if you'd just stay a week or so, you'll feel better than you ever have." There were few takers because Harris, in his zeal, was more than a touch off-putting. He'd step right into the personal space of a man, and he'd make sure he touched nearly every woman's forearms before he held their hands for a long time, insisting he "could feel what your level of health was."

More than one husband was furious enough to stalk back to his own wagon or horse and start back towards Harris with a weapon. The wives mostly just excused themselves as abruptly as was barely polite so they could go back and stop their men from doing anything stupid. Harris was convinced he had a good thing that could genuinely help people, and he was puzzled that they didn't ever seem to want to hear more about it. He may have started with pure intentions, but his hunger for a woman got the better of him eventually, and he took bolder and bolder chances with each female until the odds caught up with him.

Harris was long past his prime by the time James and Lily got there. True, it was his tent that still stood by the arroyo, but the reason the Gladstones inherited the tent, the arroyo, the spring, was because they saw him shot in the back by the last husband Harris would ever meet. He'd taken too many liberties walking the man's wife over to the arroyo and then putting his arm around her waist to lean her forward to look at the wash in the bottom. Her shriek of fear galvanized her husband into action, who, because of word of mouth along the trail, had brought his rifle along. Her husband pulled his grateful wife from Harris's arms, tramped back down the track towards the wagons to leave. They'd have gone on their way had not Harris shouted out to him, "Hell, you coulda let her holler for a minute or two, couldn't ya?"

That comment, and the rusty gurgle of laughter from Harris, turned the husband on his heel back towards a confrontation. It was brief.

Harris staggered, two bullets in him, and slumped to bleed out right near where James and Lily ended up building their sod house. The ill-tempered husband took a long look at James and Lily, deciding if they were going to be a problem that needed solving, too. James raised his hands with a disarming look, then made a shooing motion with both hands to them. Lily showed a sympathetic face to the wife, held her own hands outstretched, waved with her fingers, and smiled. Satisfied, the shooter turned, reached his truck, and drove out of the story of Gladstone.

James and Lily called it an adobe house. Not a soddie. That seemed more authentic than using a term from the prairie that they'd passed more than a month ago. "We're nearly mountain people, Lily; that's the common kind of house around here."

She didn't care; all she knew was that the tent wasn't waterproof, bug-proof, or varmint-proof, and the sooner they got in an actual building, the better.

Chapter 36

Claire and Shelly

Shelly and Claire walked slowly down the ruts of the ranch road, holding hands for a while, then dropping each other's hands when the ruts got a little wider and the stretch in their arms didn't feel natural.

"Did I ever tell you how this place started?" Shelly asked.

"What place? This road?" Claire asked back.

"No. This whole property. What they call Gladstone House."

"Oh. Nope, you didn't."

"Well, I checked into it one time when I went into town. This place used to be a holy retreat and wellness center. Do you know what those words mean?"

"Um, well, it sounds like a church, I guess."

"That's a good way of putting it. It was like church all the time. The guy who lived here wanted to help people love God, so he invited them to come and stay."

"Kind of like Hazel and Travis?" Claire asked.

"Well, not exa—" Shelly stopped, and looked at Claire.

Shelly's eyes widened, then swelled with tears. She looked up at the sky as she stopped walking. She lifted her arms halfway to her shoulders, in a beseeching way.

"I think you may be exactly right, Claire," she said softly. "I didn't see it before, but I think those two are still doing the work of the land."

"They're pretty old—they don't do much work anymore," Claire reminded her.

"Oh, I know. We have to do *everything,* huh?" Shelly smiled. "No, what I mean is that… What I mean is that *we* are the work. Hazel and Travis are here to save *us.*"

"Maybe just Hazel. Travis doesn't hear the same things that she does. The land is a good guy. It tells people what to do," Claire said simply.

"You… may be right," Shelly said, barely above a whisper. "I'm not sure how you know what that even means, cuz I sure don't know what it means. But, yeah, there's a feeling to this place that wants us to be happy, maybe?"

"I don't like to listen to it. It makes me mad," Claire said. "I want to quit talking about it."

"Of course, sweet Claire. I just wanted to tell you about how this place started. Also, that the guy who started it turned out to be a huge fake. Stole money and made bad choices," Shelly said. "We can stop talking about it and just walk, ok?"

"He must be the bad guy, then. The one I hear in the old house."

Claire skipped ahead in her rut, giving Shelly no chance to ask her what she meant by her last statement. She resolved to ask Opal about it, maybe tonight, maybe another day, maybe later rather than sooner.

The rest of the walk passed in silence. They stopped at the arroyo where they both looked down at the scoured and sculpted bottom which was still scattered with rocks and old driftwood that had wedged itself underneath rocks or roots. A purity to the scouring. They turned for Gladstone House with one accord—Claire's mind free and unburdened, Shelly's fully troubled with the rabid shift in paradigm. Her own doing.

Opal met them where the road met the farmyard.

"Hello, sweet girls. How was the walk?" Opal said with a desperate chipperness, somehow knowing.

"Oh, Mom, we had a good time! Did you know there used to be a bad man who made a church here?"

"Is that so?" Opal questioned, looking at Shelly.

Shelly offered a rueful grin. "I told her about the guy who originally started the Gladstone House. He ran a cult, back before we really called things cults."

"*Here?*"

"Oh, yeah! Right on this very ground we are standing on. The spring drew him, of course. But somehow he claimed it as his own and, well, convinced people, I guess, to live here and follow him."

"Well, you personally have to come in and help me figure out supper. I pulled some things down from the cupboards, but saw you guys coming back and escaped. You do know about me and the kitchen, right?" Opal said with a desperate twinkle in her eye.

"I do, indeed! Yes, let's see if food will help us return to at least some semblance of normal out here in the middle of nowhere," Shelly laughed.

"Can we have biscuits? Please?" Claire urged.

"That we can, little lady. That, we can."

The trio turned for the house, headed up the back steps, and into the kitchen. They moved quietly when they got inside as they saw Hazel still sleeping, curled into a ball on her side.

"Claire, go in there and put a blanket on Hazel. Quietly, now. Then pull the door almost closed but not closed, ok?" Opal said with her hand on Claire's shoulder.

"Sure, Mama. I'll be super quiet," Claire whispered as she tiptoed off. Her dusty toes made no sound on the floor but left a few tiny toe prints of desert dust, brought inside to remind them where they were.

"Now. Where's the shortening?" Shelly pondered.

Chapter 37

Claire

"Pretty soon, it will be just us, Mama," Claire said, holding her mother's hand.

Claire, when she turned five, went walking one day with Opal. Opal had taken her other times, of course, but this was the first time that Claire had actually had a thought that stopped Opal in her tracks. How many five-year-olds can make a statement that poleaxes someone?

"Out of the mouths of babes must have come from somewhere," Opal murmured to herself, softer than Claire could hear.

They had been walking along the twin ruts of the farm road on a cracking fine day in late September. Well after the heat of summer had passed, well before the snows of autumn began auditioning for the true winter show. The sun sat high and satisfied above the wild plain of desert scrub, and the girls had walked all the way to the ravine.

"It's called an arroyo, Claire."

"Arroyo," Claire repeated. She spoke clearly yet simply. Claire normally wasn't given to long speeches or even significant sentences most of the time. "What's that mean again?"

"It's the Spanish word for ravine," Opal answered. "Which is probably the French word for gully, which is another word for small canyon, which is another Spanish word."

Claire laughed, smiled at her mama, and said, "You're funny. That's too many words!"

"It is, isn't it? That's just a place where rain or a river washed away enough dirt to make a channel for it. Remember when it rained yesterday?"

"Oh, *yeah*, Mama, that was *scary*."

"Was it? Because why?"

"The *thunder*, Mama, remember?"

"Oooh, yeah, that was scary—I forgot. But we were safe in the house with Shelly and Hazel. Why were you scared?"

Claire stood, her hands on her hips, and looked severely at her mother.

"Mom, Hazel and Shelly won't be here very much longer. What happens when it is just *us*?"

"What do you mean, they won't be here very much longer?"

"Hazel is going to heaven. Travis is going with her. Shelly is going away," Claire said flatly.

"What in the… Who said that?"

"That building said so. There wasn't a person."

"Which building?" Opal held her hand to her head, flung off-kilter by her tiny girl's pitiless revelation.

"That one," Claire pointed to the old, square adobe walls that stood as the remains of the Gladstone House.

"That. Cannot. Be. True," Opal said firmly.

"Also, it said to come look at all the shiny metal in this," she said as she pointed down into the arroyo.

Opal had walked out here several times over the span of time since she and Claire had arrived—Claire as a baby, and Opal as much the same naive young woman she remained today. There had never been any 'shiny metal' of note in the arroyo, but, as she followed little Claire's chubby pointer finger, there were indeed several shiny things. They looked, to Opal, much like pieces of some sort of transportation. Metal wheels. A chrome bumper. Several long pieces of shaped wood that also had rusted metal attached to it. Uncovered by a flash flood after a long summer of dry weather that dug into the banks, perhaps.

Trouble, no matter what. Opal could feel it, whether she heard the voices in the adobe house or not. Claire's offhand comment had just heralded the apocalypse.

Chapter 38

Revelation Day

A few hours earlier, Shelly—normally the indoor gal—went for a long walk out in the scrub. All her misgivings about the origin of the property, the inconsistent memory of Travis, the truculence of Hazel about all the things she refused to talk about, flooded her senses.

She stepped carefully past the colonies of prickly pear cactus, smiling at the cheery yellow blossoms that dotted the tops of most of the pods, but still stayed within the protecting spines. It might have been warm enough for a rattler or two, but she didn't see or, more importantly, hear any. Shelly knew deep down that there was only one way to solve the puzzle that had stopped them all up; it felt like a logic puzzle did before the right solution just magically appeared. She believed they had tried the most likely of solutions and had yet to find the next level of thought that would unlock the answer.

To begin, then, it was necessary to ask the right question. It made little sense to continue wandering around in the dark, intellectually speaking, looking for the key piece of dysfunction that haunted the Gladstone House. This question, as yet unformed, drew Shelly out of the comfortable house and into the air, where she felt the distractions slide off her skin. She knew that Opal's question, "What's with the original house?", although not exactly right, contained the essence of Shelly's disquiet. Additionally, Opal repeating what Travis said to her—"We had no choice, did we?"—contained another key piece of archaeology. Arrowheads scuffed out of the dirt, offering clues to which tribe shaped them. Like that, but different. She didn't have time to decide how her quest was different or similar to the quest of a digger's—but her mind, in a self-protective effort, tried to throw her off the track.

"The question. That is the question."

Shelly finally decided that the question she needed to pose to both Travis and Hazel, along with Opal and young Claire, was this: How did James, Lily, and Nathan die? She would need to insist that Travis stop hiding behind his fake hysteria and age-addled mind. She had seen him in enough unguarded moments now to know it wasn't Alzheimer's, hardening of the arteries, or any other outdated way to describe senility. It was *cover.* It was cover for a lifetime of hiding a guilt that he never talked about, at least to anyone beyond Hazel. The trick, then, would be to get them all to the table and keep them all at the table long enough to lay out the truth that would help them all. She turned for the Gladstone House, her mind made up.

On the way back, Opal met her on the path. Opal had walked out alone, her face full of a heavy worry and tinged with grace.

"Shelly. I'm glad I found you. We—" Opal paused. "What are we going to do?"

"Hello, sweet Opal. Yes, we have a problem. I agree," she said, though Opal hadn't said anything to agree or disagree with.

"You've got a plan, then?"

"Oh, yeah. I most certainly do. I have you to thank for it, although we should have done this four years ago when you got here."

"Should've done what?"

"We need to get Hazel and Travis to come in and talk with us. And stay there until we can get to the bottom of it," Shelly said, looking at Opal. "Do you trust me?"

"I, uh, of course."

"Then come with me, make sure Claire is with us, and follow my lead."

Shelly strode back towards the farmyard, then tracked towards Travis's cabin. Opal trailed her and went into the main house, calling for Claire. Claire came skipping around the side of the house, having hopped off the rope swing that hung from the great cottonwood near the house.

"Come on in, Claire, it's time for dinner."

"I guess I can come with you—it's time, isn't it?"

"For dinner, yes."

"No, I mean, for the bigger stuff. Right?" Claire insisted.

Shelly just nodded, still uncomfortable with Claire's… whatever it was called.

"Come on, Travis, I know it's a little early for supper, but we have to talk about the tractor," Shelly said over her shoulder as she walked back towards the house.

"Well, what the heck's wrong with the tractor?" he said.

"Come on in and find out," she said flatly.

"I had that thing runnin' like a top until all these women came along and started messin' with it. Why can't they leave well enough alone and let me do the tractorin'?" he muttered as he scuffed through the farmyard.

Chapter 39

Hazel

Hazel dreamed. She lay awake, on her side on her bed, for barely two minutes. She slipped from looking at an uninhabited farm out the window to seeing her father and mother wrestling with the horse and plow without really knowing which was 'now' and which was 'memory'.

As Hazel dreamed, she felt the breeze through the rusty screen on her face, and heard her parents urging the burro to keep pulling and not stop to nip at the switchgrass in clumps across the ground they were trying to plow. Of course, Hazel never would have watched her parents plow from this bigger Gladstone House. Her dreaming brain ticked this off the list of implausibilities while continuing to wonder if they ever did get any usable land plowed with that stupid burro. Donkey. Ass. She'd forgotten which was which, genetically speaking. She did know that Cholla, the pack animal, was a right bitch when she didn't want to contribute to the cause. Which was almost always. The important piece of the dream, that her subconscious was trying to tell her, was that her parents had been happy together. They had been resolute in their plan to make this a great place to live and be a source of grace along what was then a wagon trail. Hazel watched them both laugh at the antics of Cholla, smile at each other, put a hand on each other's shoulder, and then turn back to the work with a grin.

She heard them speak—"You know, Lily, I'd be perfectly happy to move with you into one of the towns right around here. You don't need to tough it out if you're miserable," her father said, still in her dream.

"I'm not going anywhere, Mr. Gladstone. You've asked me here on this date and I love it. Besides, who wants to live in some dumb old town with idiot women to have to make conversation with?" said her mother.

"Ok, then, here we stand," Father intoned like a preacher.

Her mother laughed, swatted him with her work glove, and turned back to the plow. "Great sermon, pastor. Now could you *please* stop preaching and do some work?" she said with a laugh.

It was after that, her REM reminded her, that Travis and Nathan had come out to work with them. Still dreaming, she saw Travis pulling on Cholla's halter and Nathan pushing at the plow, muttering under his breath about being an "ass for the Lord." The character replacement made no sense and she couldn't see where her parents had gone. Her stomach fluttered and she felt a shiver of worry; the kind you get when something horrible has already taken place and you're just finding out about it and trying to catch up, attempting to quell the cognitive dissonance that comes with conflicting data input.

She trembled in her sleep on the bed, shivered, whimpered.

It's not that Claire was a being from another world or dimension or a sprite. She had never tried to explain it to either of the two adults she lived with (that weren't her mother) all her five (almost six) years of her life. It's just that she could see parts of people that, apparently, other people could not see. Hazel, for example, right now was lying on the bed curled up into a ball. But another Hazel, the *real* Hazel, sat with crossed legs right above her waist. Claire could see through this *other* Hazel to the pillows and comforter behind her. And these *other* parts never talked to Claire. She had tried when she was younger, but quit when they only smiled or frowned at her. She noticed that they did more than smile or frown now; probably always had, but her younger mind didn't recognize the different emotions. Claire made it a practice to ask her mother often about emotions and what people's faces did when they felt a certain thing.

The look on *real* Hazel right now, as that part of Hazel looked at Claire, was the same look Claire saw on the faces of animals that were dying or were about to be killed. Like a dying, sad fear. Claire took the tightly woven, yet light, wool blanket that was draped over the footboard and slowly drew it flat and up Hazel's sleeping body. Hazel's left foot twitched twice. Hazel folded her hands tightly under her chin. She moaned softly. Claire took care not to let the fringe of the blanket tickle Hazel's neck and turned that portion of the blanket back down.

She put her hand right on top of *other* Hazel's knee, patted the air it occupied, and then turned to leave the room. She pulled the door closed right up until the last two inches where it always squeaked.

Chapter 40

Claire, Shelly, and Opal

She rejoined her mother and Shelly in the kitchen, both now occupied with the mundane tasks of putting a menu together to feed five.

"Did she stay asleep?" Opal asked.

"Yep, she did. She's not ok, though," Claire said.

"What do you mean?" Shelly said, sharing a look with Opal. Shelly flicked her eyes down abruptly and fiercely at Claire, while still looking at Opal.

"Well, I mean, she maybe doesn't want to wake up," Claire said hesitantly.

"How would you know that?" Opal asked.

"Why would you think that?" Shelly said, at the same time.

"You guys wouldn't understand. Don't worry, Shelly. What's for dinner?"

The two women exchanged another look, and a shrugged shoulder, and both turned back to the task of food. Something they could at least put their minds to work on and perhaps stop the fear from bubbling too quickly over their patina of calm.

"Well, biscuits, for sure! Special request."

Claire raised her hands in triumph and glee and a huge grin split her innocent face. It was entirely possible that both Opal and Shelly just had the willies, and Claire was no part of it at all.

"Also, I'm making a huge batch of meatloaf! I've thrown all kinds of stuff in there," Shelly said with a smile. At Claire's narrowed eyes, she said, "Don't worry. The raisin experiment will *never be repeated.* I promised you then and I will always remember that promise! No raisins ever again!"

"Whew. That made it totally gross."

"Totally agree. Totally no raisins."

"Hey, you two, can you keep an eye on this stuff? I'll just go over quick and make sure that Travis is ok. I'll be back in a sec to help put everything in the oven. You don't even have to do anything!" Shelly said.

"Go on, then, Shelly—I bet we can hold the fort here for a second, right?" Opal said.

Chapter 41

Shelly and Travis

Shelly patted them both as she stepped out the door and out onto the dusty farmyard. The walk with Claire had, perhaps, shaken her more than she realized. She'd gotten a sudden chill when she thought about Travis, and the urge to go check on him was as bad as the short notice that came along with a sick stomach. She walked quickly across the yard, onto the porch, and drew up short when she saw Travis rocking with his eyes open. He didn't acknowledge her in any way, though, and he stared almost unblinkingly off at the horizon.

"Travis?"

No answer. No change in expression. The rocking of the chair slowed to nothing. His arms draped along the wooden armrests. His boot-heels stayed stuck to the floor, the toes of his boots just above the planking.

"Travis?!" she said louder.

Nothing. His eyes definitely were not blinking. She pushed him, hard, on his left shoulder with her right hand, hard enough to start the rocker up again. With a great whoosh of in-taken air, Travis came back to the present.

"What the heck was that?" he said to her. "I was hearing you, but my body seemed like it had just froze up or something. Did I say anything to you?" he asked.

"Oh my God, Travis! I thought you were dead!" Shelly said, shaking.

"Aw, hell, I ain't dead! That was weird, though, I'll give ya that much."

Shelly sat, heavily, in the other chair, her legs finally deciding to quit providing any structural support.

"This day. It's been a little too much for me, I'm afraid."

"For *you*? How do you think it's been for me and Hazel?" he complained. "I'm not one to say 'I told you so' but, for the love of Pete, I told you this was a lousy idea."

"Boy, you can say that again," she moaned. "Well, anyway, I just came to make sure you're ok. Which you are. So I'm gonna go back and get supper to cooking. I'll send one of the girls over to get you when we're ready, ok?"

"That's a grand idea, right there, Miss Shelly. Now, don't you worry! We old coots are gonna be just fine."

"You just keep breathing, old man."

Shelly hugged him briefly and fiercely as she stood back up to go walk over to the house. He raised one arm halfway up to hug her back, but she was already pulling away and turning for the house. He continued to sit in the chair, wishing he didn't have to pee so badly and he could just doze off right there like he loved to do.

Chapter 42

Shelly

Shelly, true to her word, came right back to the main house through the back door after the incident with Travis not-exactly-breathing. She saw that Opal and Claire were sitting in the front room and decided to leave them alone.

What she would have given to share a moment like that, on a couch, with her own mother? Long forgotten back east. Her stubbornness initially dominated and resisted any attempts Hazel tried to get Shelly to patch things up.

"I'll write back if they write to me," she'd said to Hazel.

"But, honey, how will they know where to find you?" Hazel would say, every time.

Shelly had an obtuse notion that, since she never got her suitcase off the bus, that the bus company would return it to the only owner that was indicated in the case. The only thing identifying the case was her mother's Bible, so Shelly just assumed they'd return it to her. In point of fact, though Shelly had no way of finding that out, the Trailways people did exactly that.

"We're not sure how your case ended up on our bus line to Las Vegas, New Mexico, but we feel the best course of action is to return it, at our cost, to the name and address we found in some of the personal effects inside the case. Please contact us if we can be of any further service…" etc., etc.

Shelly's parents accepted the rather large package, delivered by truck. Her mother opened it when her husband was still away at the pulp mill. She put her hand over her mouth to stifle the sobs forcing their way through her pursed lips. However, by the time her husband—Shelly's father—had come home, she'd thrown out the packaging, spread the few clothing items among her own things, and put her Bible back into the carved family Bible box that sat on the metal shelf underneath the television in the living room. They both had other Bibles that they used for their morning prayers and devotions, and she was pretty sure her husband didn't know that she'd sent her own old Bible with Shelly when she left.

A few months later, when her husband gruffly asked if "she'd heard from *your* daughter," her mother just slowly shook her head and said nothing. She always vowed that she would do some investigating one day and figure out where, exactly, on the bus route Shelly had stopped. But, as the months passed, one thing or another took her attention and, by the time her husband took sick from cancer and died after a few months, she had abandoned the idea altogether. She called it her penance that she would have to live her last few years alone and unloved, except by well-meaning but gossip-driven church people who brought the same old casseroles to her door far too often. Those visits, too, she counted as penance for not fighting more to keep her daughter with her.

In any case, Shelly knew none of her mother's troubles, and wouldn't have much sympathy for her, anyway. They kicked *her* out. And it wasn't like she was *hiding* at Gladstone; it would take a detective about five phone calls to find her, if they wanted to. So Shelly, long ago, had resigned herself to being an orphan with parents. And she was fine with it, until she stood and looked at the obvious and clarifying love that Claire and Opal had for each other. Strength in numbers and a welcome port in a storm.

Chapter 43

Claire and Opal

While Shelly was out, Opal took Claire's hand and walked out of the kitchen and into the front room where there was a big couch—Hazel always called it a divan. Opal led her to this piece of furniture and pulled her down next to her. They sat in silence for a minute or two. Claire glanced at her mom, but then turned her attention to the different pieces in the room. Opal alternated her gaze between Claire's face and the old tintype pictures on the walls. Several of the pictures were of the titillating variety—photos of voluptuous, fleshy women taking a sponge bath back in olden times. They looked naked, but most of their actual 'privates' were artfully covered. A sponge here, a fern there, a draped towel in another. These were part of the charm that people noticed when they stopped to come in for a break from the road. The glass counter held the fresh bread samples, and baskets sat on either end of the counter. Empty now, but they'd fill them with breads and jams and sometimes even fresh vegetables that they'd just picked from the garden.

The two front windows, wide double-paned ones, were closed. They did, for the most part, leave them up an inch or two, especially when it was a mild day or when the house had gotten hot from the oven baking all that bread. Sheer white cotton curtains, fringed with lace, hung straight down from the top of the windows. They had long ago installed old-fashioned lights that mimicked hurricane lamps, although they usually only used them on sale days. They had fluorescent lights running right down the center of the ceiling which they used far more often. The bulbs were cheap, the light was better to dust and sweep with, and they didn't have to worry about the old bulbs needing replacing. It was a business decision at first, but then the women decided to continue conserving the old-fashioned ones for 'special occasions'. Like when they could make money.

"Claire? Can you tell me what Shelly was talking about? The walk you guys took?"

"I know you told me not to talk about the voices, Mom. I remember that. I'm usually pretty good at not talking about it. But, it just seemed like she really needed to know," Claire offered.

"Yeah, but honey, you know they don't understand what we hear that they can't, right?"

"You've told me that a million times."

"It's not like it's *weird*. I think we, you and me, just can hear a little more of the spiritual world than most people. And, what do we know, anyway? We never go into town, we don't go see other people, or families, or tourists. Just who-ever stops here. And Hazel, Travis, Shelly."

"I know. I just don't understand why we have to keep it secret."

"Yeah, I'm not sure I understand that, either. I just think they'd start to get mad at us or suspicious."

"Like we are able to make things happen to them?" Claire said slowly.

"Maybe like that, yeah. Maybe just that they'd look at all the time to see if we are 'getting a vision'. Which is dumb."

"Yeah. It doesn't work that way."

"Right," Opal said. "But, tell me again, what did you and Shelly talk about out on the road?"

"All's she said was some dumb old guy made a church place, and people came, and he turned out to be a bad man."

"And did you say anything to her?"

"All's I said was the spring was a good guy."

"Well, that's not so bad. Is that all?"

"And I said the bad guy must be the one talking to me in the old house," Claire said defensively.

"Oh, Claire. I told you. Don't tell anyone about that. They just won't get it! They'll get all jumpy about it."

"I *know*. I couldn't *help* it. It just slipped out."

"She got jumpy then, didn't she?"

"Yes," she said with a pout. "I'm just a kid, Mom. How am I supposed to remember when to tell the truth and when to not bring it up?"

Opal, in answer, pulled her close to her on the couch and hugged her tightly, burying her face in Claire's long blonde hair.

"You're choking me!"

"I'm sorry, sweetest. I can't help it."

Claire let her keep hugging her, though. Pretty soon their breathing slowed and steadied as they leaned back on the puffy cushions framed by the dark, curved wood pieces of the couch. Claire, playing the game they'd played ever since babyhood, lightly pinched her mother's nose closed. Opal pretended to panic, then opened her mouth with a laugh and reached over to pinch Claire's nose shut. They took turns doing this until they got bored. Then they simply sat, arm in arm, thinking about nothing in particular, wondering what the rest of the evening would bring.

Chapter 44

Hazel, Opal, and Claire

Earlier that afternoon, Opal had convinced Hazel to come sit on the porch with her, a few hours before the 'Revelation', as Opal and Claire would soon refer to it.

"Don't you want us to know the whole story before we have to take over everything?" Opal asked.

"I'm not sure why I'm gonna tell you this whole story. I guess I just need someone to know how all this started so you can judge how it turns out," Hazel said.

She was sitting in her rocker on the back porch in the afternoon sun, looking out over the whole of Gladstone.

"This all started back before I was born, and by the time I was old enough to pay attention, we had settled here for good, mother was sad as all hell, and father just kept working harder, hoping it would turn for the good for us," she said.

"You're doing the right thing, Hazel," Opal said. "We want to remember all this while you can still tell us."

Opal was a slip of a girl, and they had all raised her baby Claire to age six right along with her right here on Gladstone.

"I still think it's way better to just let all this lie under the dirt Travis and I buried it in," she said. But gently.

Opal patted Hazel's arm, all spotted and frail and thinned by at least 80 years of desert living, that lay along the rail of the rocker. They let the afternoon settle a bit, watched the sun change the shadows of the cholla cactus at the edge of the yard.

"Ok, well. I was baby number two. That's why Mama was so sad. Baby number one didn't make it. When I was born, we still lived in that adobe house that Father built. He built that very first thing, even before Uncle Travis and Uncle Nathan came out here. When those two got here, they all built this house, then the house over there that Travis still stays in."

Hazel gestured towards the long and narrow building on the far side of the road. The back porch they both sat on was the main Gladstone House on Gladstone Property. No one except those five who lived there bothered to call it much of anything, although the bus route map read, "Gladstone—ten minutes for convenience and prairie shopping."

"Claire, I'm pretty sure I don't have to tell you this. Opal, I haven't decided if you have the sight or not."

"I know already, but you should tell Mama," Claire said.

Hazel lifted her tired head, turned to fully face Opal, and opened her eyes wide. "Opal, this place, Gladstone, speaks to me. It's a thin place. A place where, I don't know, I can understand better than most places what people need."

"A thin place? What does that mean?" Opal said.

"I'm sure there's a real word for it, back in some holy place where all they do is study how to get close to God or whatever they worship. All I know is that I can feel what's right and wrong. When I'm here. On Gladstone. Especially out at the spring."

"What about the old adobe, Hazel?" young Claire asked.

"I scurry by that place, Claire, and you should, too. Nothing but trouble from that voice," Hazel said grimly.

"Are you saying those places are haunted? That you hear voices out loud?" Opal asked cynically.

Claire put her little hand on her mom's hand. "Mama, no. It's not like that. It's more like a drawing. With a pencil. A picture of what should happen to bring happiness."

"I've never thought I'd heard voices, either, Opal, but, to me, it's more like a moving picture. Scene one is the problem, then the rest of the scenes are about how to make it better. Like a flip book!" Hazel said suddenly.

"And you already know all this, Claire?" Opal said.

"Mama. Remember? It's why I know what you are dreaming about. *Remember?*"

"I worry about your dreams, too, Opal. I surely don't want you to go back to Taos to find Claire's daddy, but she might be right—you may have to," Hazel said.

Opal slumped back in her porch rocker. She hadn't realized that every waking moment she had not one but two monitors that took stock of her spirit, either rooting for her or wishing she'd turn away.

"So you can read all my thoughts? All the time?" Opal said.

"Oh, no. It's not like that. It's more like a—well, it's hard to explain. And, anyway, we can talk more about that tonight. I'm too tired to repeat myself," Hazel said with a grin. "I need to go rest for a minute."

Chapter 45

Hazel

Hazel came back to consciousness slowly, so very slowly. She felt a paralysis in her legs, and, as she tried to move her arms, realized they didn't want to move either. She had to tilt her head down, still sideways on the pillow to see if her feet were actually moving, or it was all her mind convincing her. Tricking her. Her left foot, still laying atop her right one, ankle bones grating against each other, twitched. Relieved, she rolled her foot in a small circle, then moved her leg back and forth on the hinge of her knee. She straightened her leg from her hip, moved it back and forth, a small gasp of pain when she flexed her quadriceps (which used to be so strong! She could hike all day). She pressed her left arm down into the mattress right in front of her chest, and pushed herself up to a sitting position. Her hair had flattened on the pillow side, and her reflection in the window glass made her look like one of Kahlo's uneven women.

She looked through the glass then, and out into the scrub, wondering if her parents had finished the plowing, or the boys had finished. That's what she called Travis and Nathan, the boys. They felt more like brothers than they did uncles; she never did quite understand the gap between her father and the two brothers. When they came out west, it just seemed like they were already-grown adults, rather than two scared boys trying to front their way past real adults, at railway stations, at general stores, at livery corrals. As the murky fog of her dream cleared, she remembered that her parents and Nathan had been long dead. The talk at the table had brought their memories back out of her long-term storage and to her forebrain, wanting her to deal with them more fully.

She lunged to her feet and staggered one step to the left toward the doorway. She straightened, fluffed her hair with both hands, and thought maybe she'd wash her hair later in the evening rather than wait until Friday, like usual. Immediately she scoffed at her 'putting on airs', as her mother used to say. "We only need wash once a week, Hazel, you know that," her mother said. And then her father would lecture her about how much work it took to heat the pan of water on the wood stove, and that wood needed cutting, and that they needed to save for the winter, and that someone would have to go fill the pan at the well, and didn't she realize how much work it took to run a farm?

A small sob caught in Hazel's throat; she wasn't sure why. She raised her chin, set her jaw, and stepped back into the kitchen.

"Well, hello there, sweet Shelly. Have I missed my chance to help with supper?" she said as she moved to the center of the kitchen.

"Hazel—welcome back! Boy, the number of times I've seen you take a nap in the late afternoon I could count on one hand. Maybe one finger. Are you feeling better?" Shelly said warmly.

"I've had the strangest dreams, since you ask."

"Oh? What of? And, no, no need to help with supper. I have a meatloaf in and some biscuits keeping them company in there. I was just about to rouse everyone to come in."

"Many thanks for taking over. I was simply exhausted, which, you're right, isn't much like me."

Hazel sat in her chair at her customary place, rubbed one finger lightly over the pattern on her plate, remembering how long they'd had this set. Mother had brought it with them when they moved out here.

"Perhaps I'll wait for the others to tell you about my dream," she hesitated.

"I think that's a fine idea, Hazel," Shelly said in that careful, respectful way one often used to talk to a confused, shaky elder.

Shelly, to this point, hadn't really considered Hazel to be elderly, but when she came back into the kitchen after her rest, she looked like she'd aged years. It called to Shelly's mind the oddity of Dorian Gray. Something about paint making a person older or younger, or a mirror reflecting true age, or a haunting that robbed years from a person.

"Stay right here, Hazel. I'll go get the girls."

"I'll do that," Hazel murmured.

Shelly walked through the partition curtain and approached Claire and Opal on the couch.

"Opal? Claire? Could you come join us for supper? It's about time. Well, by the time you freshen up I'll have the food out, anyway."

"Sure," Opal said, sitting straight and stretching mightily, arms pushed straight as if holding the ceiling from collapsing. Claire also sat up and rubbed her eyes, looking blearily up at Shelly.

"Want me to go get Travis, Shelly?" Claire asked.

"I'd like that, dear Claire," Shelly said, before remembering that Travis had been in that weird fugue state when she went back there a little while ago.

"Hey, though, be careful not to startle him; he might have dozed off, too. It seems like it's been a tiring day."

"Oh, I know. I'll be real careful. But he always remembers me so I never scare him. I'll tell him about the biscuits and he'll come right with me," Claire said, and smiled.

Chapter 46

Revelation Day

Shelly sighed, and turned back to the kitchen, where she knew she could make food her comfort and mission. She dug her hands into the meatloaf mixture, turned it and pressed it a few times, then placed it in the center of the glass cooking dish. She pushed it down to widen it almost to the edges of the pan. After she washed her hands of the greasy mess, she sliced two onions and placed a half each in each corner of the baking dish, just for the aroma. She double-checked the oven temperature, heard from an echo of Hazel —"it'll burn at 400!"—and then turned to the biscuit project. Biscuits always brought joy to people, no matter how she made them.

As she turned out the drop biscuits, she thought about the loose ends of the conversation they'd all had earlier that afternoon. What else did she want to know? What else did she need to know? How much more stress could both Travis and Hazel take? Travis's weird fugue state and Hazel's uncharacteristic nap bothered her. Nevertheless, she resolved to be determined in her pursuit of the loose ends of the conversation. She got the dishes out, the good China this time, and began to set the table for supper. They each had a customary place, and she set the places with that in mind. Claire liked the little tiny silverware; a small spoon and what was really a pickle fork, and she never used a knife. Hazel liked a big tablespoon and always exchanged her normal teaspoon for one, if, by chance, the table setter didn't do it that way at the outset. Travis ate everything with a fork, except for soup. He'd use a spoon for about half the bowl, then he'd slurp the rest or sop it up with whatever bread they'd have. There was always bread; no self-respecting farm table would be without bread, after all. Shelly folded cloth napkins in triangles and placed the long side underneath and parallel to the knives. A simple, clear water glass sat at the two o'clock position of each plate.

It was a sunny late afternoon at Gladstone House, and the light slanted in the rear windows with warmth, but with no malice. A breeze waxed and waned through the screens of the open windows. Like many early summer days on the high desert, the temperature inside with a breeze was just right. The kitchen table, two chairs per side and one chair per end, had seen years of meals and family business meetings.

After a time, they had all gathered at the supper table. The food was laid on, serving dishes all matching, serving spoons all matching. Freshly brewed iced tea in the pitchers. There was a moment where no one talked because they were all taking turns filling their plates with meatloaf, biscuits, green beans with bacon, and bread baked fresh only one day ago. They ate in contented silence. Hazel sat on one long side of the table, facing away from the center of the house and towards the open windows and the sun of the day. Opal and Claire sat across from her. When Shelly came in, she stood subtly by the chair at the head of the table. This chair was normally where Travis sat, but she motioned him around her and pulled the chair out for him that was next to Hazel. Shelly had decided that she needed to look like she was running the meeting, and for that she needed to sit at the head of the table. There was an uncertain moment when Travis hesitated and looked at the opposing 'head of the table' chair, but, in the end, he sat next to his niece. Hazel and Travis looked alert but not suspicious; it wasn't so rare that they all gathered to talk about one issue or another that they'd gotten wind of the box canyon they'd both walked into. Nor had Shelly lit the evidentiary fire at the mouth of the canyon yet to keep them there.

Finally, looking at each face around the table, Shelly took a breath.

"So. I wanted to say a few things. And I know you may want to stop me right away, but I ask you to please just let me finish. We have plenty of time," she said mildly.

"Go ahead, dear, we'll try," Hazel said.

"Ok. Well, first, I'm sorry I had to bring it all up. I just—" She stopped, but held a finger up. "I just needed to know how this all came about. Second, I'm still not clear on a few things and, even if it makes things worse, I need to ask more questions."

All five of them sat in place at the table, Travis and Claire eating heartily, the three women either picking at food or pushing bits around their plates. Hazel's mouth was set in almost a grimace, her lips drawn tightly together as if blowing through a straw. Opal merely showed a despairing frown, like she knew this would be their last peace.

"Before you ask all that, Shelly, could I say something?" Opal asked.

Feigning impatience and shock, Shelly said, "Gee, I made it three sentences! No, I'm kidding, please, Opal, go ahead."

"I just want you to know, Travis and Hazel," and she looked at both of them in turn, "how damned grateful we are that you took us in when you did. I think, no, I *know* you saved our lives that day. No matter how this turns out or what we all say or how we all react or what we think we need to take back or do over, I want you to hear that 'thank you' loud and clear. I want that 'thank you' to be the first and last thing you think about each day. Ok?"

"I heartily agree with you, Opal. And I wish I would have started with that, too," Shelly said. "You've always been so good about loving."

Shelly looked at Opal with a face full of emotion, suffused yet not crying. Travis kept chewing, and smiled around his fork as he kept his mouth full of supper. He finished a mouthful, then said,

"Hell, I ain't usually one to talk a whole lot. Don't expect me to change now. This afternoon's tales was all true, but don't think I'm gonna get in the habit of re-tellin' all the history I remember. Mebbe if you keep feeding me like this, I might," he laughed. He took another bite. "I've told you before, and I'll keep sayin' it. Hazel made all them decisions about takin' you poor waifs in. She gets all the credit as far as I'm concerned."

"It's great to have us all together this fine afternoon for supper, isn't it?" Shelly began again.

Opal rolled her eyes and smirked. Claire picked at her napkin, waiting for the food to be served. But knowing there was more; a greater necessity of purpose.

"I needed to get us all together because I'm confused about a few things," Shelly said firmly.

"What'd you say about the tractor? That's what I'm worried about," Travis said. "If you ain't got nothin else to talk about, I'd best get out there and check into that."

"No, Travis, you stay here. The tractor isn't our biggest concern right now."

"How the heck are we supposed to plow if—"

"I mean it. The tractor's fine. I lied, ok?" Shelly said.

"You lied? I don't like that. I don't like it one bit," Hazel said, declaratively.

"Yes, let's talk about lying," Opal said.

"Opal, hang on. Let me get there," Shelly cautioned.

"What's that supposed to mean?" Hazel said, a flush rising from the base of her throat.

Shelly shifted in her seat. She looked directly at Travis, then at Hazel, with as much love as she could muster. She opened her eyes, and tried to project an open heart to both of them. She uncrossed and lowered her arms. Spread them wide along the table.

"Hazel and Travis, you two saved my life 24 years ago. I fully and freely and thankfully admit that. Had you not let me stay when I walked off down the road way back then, I'd not be alive today," she said, suffused with feeling.

"Well, now, honey, you know we—" Travis started.

"Please. Let me finish. This won't be easy for me, or for Opal, to get all the way through. I need your word on something—can I have it?"

"It depends what it is," Hazel said, her arms now crossed and her cheeks red.

"It's nothing bad. We aren't leaving. We just need you to be honest. And to not get up and walk out. And to not fake senility." Shelly laid her hand gently on Travis's arm as she said this, smiling at him.

"You know about that?" he asked.

"Oh, Travis. You had me fooled with all that drool, but not for long," Opal laughed. "I just wondered why you were doing it."

"I'll stay. Hazel?" Travis said simply, then looked at Hazel.

"Yes. Here I am. What is it?" she replied.

Shelly took a deep breath, exhaling down the table, thinking perhaps the hardest part was already over. How wrong that would turn out to be.

"When Opal got here, five and some years ago, she—"

"I got here then, too!" Claire said, raising her hand.

"Ah. Yes, sweet Claire, you came here, *too*," Shelly corrected.

"As I said, Opal got here and she found that old building. Remember that day?" Shelly asked.

Hazel nodded. Travis dipped his chin once, then again. Neither spoke.

"Opal's question that day was 'What's the story with this old building?' or something like that. And then you guys told her that's the original building where you, Hazel, lived with your parents. James and Lilah, right?"

"Lily. James and Lily."

"Right, sorry. Which underscores my point. Why don't we ever talk about them? Why wouldn't you tell us more about them? Where are the pictures? Where are the journals, the letters, the, I don't know... mementoes?" Shelly asked.

Hazel reached out her left hand and snaked it into Travis's hand. Like a child, trying not to be afraid of a bad dream. Travis took her hand into his calloused paw and patted her engulfed hand gently with his other. He cleared his throat.

"Remember when I told you they died? Six months after I got here with Nathan?" Travis said slowly. He glanced at Hazel, who shrugged one shoulder, and said, "Remember that story, Shelly?"

"I do."

A tear tracked down Hazel's cheek. The tear ran down into each crack, climbed back out to reach the next, and left a little bit of moisture in each arroyo on its way.

"We've never told the real story to anyone. *Anyone*," he said. "I've told so many half-truths about it over the years, that I'll have to concentrate to get it right again."

"And we certainly didn't talk about it with each other, until that day Opal asked about the old house," Hazel added. "Different versions or not, I bet it's never far from your thoughts, either, is it, Travis?"

"What could be so bad?" Shelly asked, gently. So gently. So much love.

"How *bad* could it be?" Hazel said, indignantly. "You know *nothing*, little girl."

"Now, Hazel, she's not a little girl. You know that. None of us are little anymore. We need to tell them. They've already figured out far too much."

"I can't bear it. I just can't."

"You've got to, Hazel. You're strong; you've done it once. One more time, ok?"

Hazel simply sat in her wooden chair, the carving on the back of the chair mimicking the grief lines across her face. Shelly hadn't realized it until that moment. They weren't laugh lines or frown lines. They were grief lines.

"We love you," Opal said. "We are never telling anyone. We are never leaving. At least we don't want to, and we hope you don't kick us out. We just know something's wrong, and we want to know what it is. So we can help, I guess," she finished lamely.

"Opal's right. We are as good as family. Better than family because we are still here," Shelly said, then clapped her hand over her mouth. "Was that mean? I didn't intend it that way!"

Hazel smiled, tired and serene. "No, love, that's not mean. You don't have a mean bone in your body. I know— *we* know—what you're saying."

"I agree—you girls are the best thing that ever happened to us," Travis offered, laying his hand, palm up, on the table. "We'd-a been dead years ago if we'd-a had to look after ourselves."

"So what we are saying is you deserve the truth. Even if you may *want* to leave after you hear it," Hazel finished. "Go on ahead, Travis. You start."

Chapter 47

Revelation Day

And, just like that, the years, almost 70 of them, stripped away. Travis's voice firmed up, he sat a little straighter, his rheumy eyes cleared, then stared back into time.

"I was 15. Hazel was eight. We had no earthly idea he was insane," he started, raising his hand to Shelly, who'd already gotten a confused look on her face.

"I'll get there, hon, just hang on. Anyways, Hazel's parents, James and Lily, had the kindest hearts of anyone I'd ever met. James was my brother. They were both *way* kinder than Mother and Father had been back east. Mother and Father allowed me and Nathan to come west, but they were pretty mean about it. They basically said don't come back. So… I had no alternate plan even if this New Mexico thing didn't work out. I'll tell you the truth, I was hoping to come out here alone because Nathan, at the time back east, had started to turn. More than a little."

"I never liked him," Hazel said.

"You didn't? I didn't know that," said Travis.

"What do you mean, 'started to turn'?" Shelly asked.

"Well, I couldn't very well tell you or my father, could I? He's family," Hazel said quietly.

"I guess not. But we did a lot of things too late in the game, didn't we? That's just one more to add to the pile. And, I'm gettin' there, Shelly."

Travis shifted back to the center of the table, folded his hands, and looked at Shelly, Opal, and Claire in turn. Hazel continued to sit, but made a moue of pain as she shifted slowly on the hard wooden chair.

"It was always Nathan. Nathan was the crazy one. And I don't mean over-enthusiastic, or hot-and-bothered, or even zealous. All those things can be tempered," Travis admitted. "I mean he was insane. Somewhere between St. Louis and Gladstone he lost his mind. Do you remember what he always said, Hazel? Nearly every hour?"

"Oh, yes. I remember all too well. He'd say, 'The Lord Almighty has a Purpose for me, and I am here to fulfill Him.' He'd say that all the time. It's chilling as I think on it now," she murmured. "He acted like that one prophet in the Old Testament who said God would judge us all and deliver us all to our just rewards, and then a whole bunch of people died in the Bible story."

"Exactly. 'I am a Servant of the Lord God Almighty and I am here to do His Will.'" Travis shook his head back and forth, slowly, disbelievingly. "I mean, he's not the first fired-up preacher to wander through these parts. This high desert made a *lot* of men crazy—never saw a woman do it, though—and they'd tramp around here without shoes talking about the wilderness. At least until a rattler got them or they got enough cactus spines in them to get infected and then get the gangrene and wander off to die under some rock."

"So, what happened? What did Nathan do?" Opal asked. "I remember you said, 'We didn't have any choice.'"

"Nathan killed my parents," Hazel said flatly. "They didn't die from any disease. He just flat out killed them."

Travis snuffled loudly, and the women realized he'd been silently weeping for a while. He dragged his arm across his nose roughly, then wiped his eyes with an old handkerchief he'd pulled from his back pocket.

"That's when I shoved my hunting knife up into his head," Travis said. "He came to me; said he'd made a mistake. He walked me out to the old adobe where he'd lain James and Lily out after he suffocated them. Hazel had already been there, seen them, ran off into the arroyo."

He took another two breaths, breathing out through pursed lips and making a hissing sound.

"He told me that God told him to do it, and that the 'Lord Almighty would breathe breath back into them once their sin was removed.' I just looked at him like he was a rabid coyote; I couldn't help it. That was a mistake. To show him my true feelings, I mean. He was about a second away from jumping me, I could tell. We'd grown up together and I remembered his hair-trigger temper and his all-or-nothing solutions to problems. And there was no way I was leaving Hazel alone with him with all three of us dead."

"And thank God for that," Hazel said.

"Yeah. It was him or me. So I shoved my hunting knife into his skull under his chin. He grabbed my arms as soon as he saw me thrust, but his brain shut down right away."

"All over but the shouting, as they say," murmured Hazel.

Chapter 48

Revelation Day

Opal and Shelly sat in horrified silence. Claire still sat at the table, forgotten momentarily. She had a look of profound emotion on her face, but it looked more complex than horror. There was a glint in her eye, and fascination etched her forehead.

"So—you killed a bad guy, right, Uncle Travis?" Claire asked.

"Oh my God, Claire—I forgot you were sitting with us!" Opal shouted.

"It's too late now," Travis said. "I knew she was here. She needs to hear this, too. You wanted it this way."

"I had no idea that—"

"You insist we tell you a tale that we've kept secret for forever and now you want us to take it back because it's too rough for young Claire?" Travis said. "You don't get to ask for the truth and have it be whitewashed."

"Ask for the rain and reap the whirlwind, is what this is," Hazel said, with no pity. "I'm sure you'll find a way to make this digestible to her. She's a precocious girl."

Opal held her head in her hands, shaking like a leaf. Shelly resolutely put her arm over on Opal's shoulder, patting her.

"Now, Claire, are you ok with this grown-up talk at the table?" Shelly asked Claire gently.

"Oh, sure, Aunt Shelly. I just wanted to know how come Nathan turned into a bad man. I need to learn how to kill the bad man, too," she said.

"What?" Opal said, through her hands.

"Well, that's what we are finding out about him, Claire. Sometimes good people turn into bad people. That's what we're asking Travis and Hazel about," Shelly added.

"I know," Claire said simply.

Hazel, exhausted, said, "Go on, Travis. Finish the story. Tell them the rest. I can't take it much longer." Her face had taken on a sickly sheen to it, sweat laid on top of pale. Travis's leg had begun to tremble under the table, which made the liquid in the lemonade pitcher tremble as if a mighty herd of bison were passing in the distance.

"He died right there in front of me. I laid his body next to James and Lily, then went to find Hazel. I didn't want a fourth death that night. It was a full moon, so she stood out clearly in her white nightgown on the edge of the arroyo.

I was worried she was going to jump."

"I wasn't going to jump."

"I had no way of knowing, so I ran to her and called her name and grabbed her around the middle. She hardly resisted. Really was more of a rag doll than anything."

"I was in shock."

"I carried her back to the adobe. Set her on her feet. Made her look at all three bodies."

"Which I did *not* want to do."

"I said it was important for her to know that we were safe now. The bad man was dead, too. I mean, I was 15, for God's sake. I had no idea what to do. There was no sheriff. At least not that night."

"We were on our own."

"We could've gone into Clayton in the morning and asked for help. But who was going to let two kids stay on that property without writing a letter somewhere for legal advice about what to do?"

"We didn't want to leave."

"As we stood there, crying and holding hands, I think it was Hazel who said it first. I just looked at her then and asked her to say that again."

"I told him that we needed to get rid of the bodies."

"It was right then that Hazel became the leader of our little band of two. It's still weird, but inspiring, to see how much steel burnt right into her backbone that night," Travis said.

"Well, I didn't want to leave. I didn't know any other life. Or at least I didn't remember any other life. I'd been a kid when we showed up, and I was probably still a kid. But I knew what I wanted, and I could see the only path to keeping that. I told Travis we needed to burn the house with Nathan in it. And we needed to find a place to bury Mama and Daddy," Hazel related, her voice, too, now much younger and firmer as she remembered.

"Of course I asked her why make all that work for ourselves?"

"If someone asks, we can say that they got sick. But Nathan had a hole in his head and there was blood all over, so we couldn't bury him just in case. Plus, three people dead in one fire just seemed too chancy."

"So I hoisted Nathan's body over my shoulder and walked him down to the old house."

"Don't tell me you just threw his body in there? Was that the pork smell that still makes you sick, Hazel?" Shelly said.

"That's what I told him to do, and, after he stripped the clothes off him, that's what he did. It was a full moon night and we had four or five hours of night left," Hazel said grimly. "Then we hauled Mama and Daddy to over near the cottonwood. Dug for a while. Put them right next to each other wrapped in one sheet. And, yes, Shelly—I'll never forget that smell."

Hazel turned to Travis. "You missed a lot of what your brother did, Travis," she said. "I was good and sick of him anyway, before he killed my parents. If you hadn't killed him, I would've. Not sure how. He was hard to catch unawares."

"I at least knew that much—why I killed him right then and there. He'd-a killed me if I hadn't."

"We lit the place on fire with kerosene dumped all over. We barely had enough for the beds and furniture to burn well. You know… a fire needs to be hot to burn up a body," Hazel said quietly.

At that, Opal pushed away from the table, strode quickly to the kitchen sink, and turned the water on with a fierce movement. She pressed her palms into the counter and lifted herself up on her tiptoes as she stared out the window. Claire stayed seated at the table, swinging her legs back and forth in her chair. She didn't look at all stressed, rather like she was at story time at a local library—if she knew what that was. Shelly slumped in her chair at the head of the table. A moderator overtaken by events that had spun out of her control.

Chapter 49

Revelation Day

"I don't know where we go from here," Shelly said. "I had no idea this was what you'd been hiding."

"Well, of course, you didn't. We've been *hiding it,* after all," Hazel exclaimed. "You asked, we decided, and here you go. Now it's your burden, too."

"Here's where we go. Everyone take a few minutes to themselves, recover, think, wonder, marvel—all those good words," Opal said. "Then, we can sit back down here and sift through the wreckage and see if we have any more questions or answers to any of this. Then I say we leave it alone. Just like you two have done for all these years."

"I agree. Now we know," Shelly said after she thought for a minute. "I, for one, can already tell you that I'm staying right here, if you'll have me. I've got no desire to start seeing the world out there past Gladstone." But even as Shelly said that, she wondered if that was true.

"My hips are aching, that's for sure. Maybe I'll just step outside for a breath of fresh air, if you don't mind," Hazel said.

"I need to go see a man about a horse," Travis said, rising from his chair.

"Can I go with you and see the horse?" Claire said brightly.

"He means he has to pee, Claire," Opal laughed.

"Oh. I don't want to watch you pee. I just want to see the horse," Claire pouted.

"Honey, there's no horse."

They all pushed away from the table, stood, and sought their own counsel in the agreed-upon quiet of the evening. Hazel, suddenly exhausted, turned from the doorway and shuffled straight to her bedroom and laid down on her side, facing the window. Travis heaved himself up from his chair with his hands on his knees and walked out the back door. He continued to his own cabin, rounding the corner and out of sight. Shelly smoothed her gray and wiry hair back from her forehead, held her hand out to Claire, and tilted her head outside. Claire got up happily from her chair and took Shelly's hand. Opal, then, was left alone in the kitchen.

Opal stared off into space out the window. Her mind registered Travis walking across her field of vision, and she subconsciously tracked Shelly and Claire walking south on the ranch road holding hands. What struck her most was how hard she had worked to escape her nightmare back in Taos, only to have landed here where, in all its pitiless review, the situation was and had been much worse. Worse both in act and in resolution; the lack of resolution, that it. This story felt lifted out of a time period more than a hundred years earlier than when it actually happened.

Opal tried to calculate what year they were talking about. Although it felt like the 1850s, she was pretty sure they said it all happened during the Great Depression of the 1930s. Why in the world did the brothers ride here on horses then? One horse, did he say? Did he say? She couldn't remember, and she didn't trust herself to remember even to ask.

She slowly sank back into a chair in the kitchen, gently placing her splitting head in her hands.

Chapter 50

The Fire

When they regathered at the table, Hazel didn't speak. She didn't have to. She merely reached her hands out, one to Shelly, one to Opal. They laid their hands atop hers, and Claire added hers to the pile, too. She had to half-stand up from her chair for her arm to reach.

"Ok, go on then, Shell," Opal said.

Shelly paused, drew her hand back to her lap, wiped a single tear.

"Tell me again how the fire started. In the old adobe or sod house," she said slowly.

"I started it."

Hazel had shifted in her chair and spoken as if from a great distance.

"Travis had taken most of his clothing off—Nathan's I mean, not his own. My heart just about broke when I watched him walk down that road after he put Nathan in the adobe. He didn't seem heavy at all to him. And then I was stuck there. Looking down at my dead parents."

"You watched me walk off, huh?" Travis mused.

"Yeah. And then I just couldn't bear to make you come back and deal with the rest of the mess, too. I'd never wanted to feel helpless, even in little things. Let alone something like this. So, I took down both the hurricane lamps and dumped the oil all over—" At this she stopped, looked down.

"Take your time, Hazel," Shelly offered.

Her eyes blazed and settled on Shelly.

"I'll thank you to keep your advice to yourself. You asked for all this horrid truth, and we'll give it to you. You've already trespassed, in my opinion, and I don't want your approval or urging to continue to answer! Clear?" she said.

Shelly had no answer but an anguished look as an apology.

"I put one of the hurricane lamps back right near the doorway, then ran the door over it so the glass broke. I poured the rest of the bottle of lamp oil they kept in a corner over the beds and the small table. Then I threw a match on the whole godforsaken place. It sputtered a little, then caught, then forced me outside. The roof poles eventually caught and collapsed and took the tops of two of the walls with them."

"By the time I walked back up the road, it was a roaring fire. I couldn't tell the color of the smoke, but it felt greasy," Travis said.

"Like pork. Just like pork," Hazel said with both infinite sadness and pitiless narration.

Again, they all sat in a silence that refused all spoken thoughts of conciliatory salve. A bond, then, forged in the quiet, and acknowledged as unbreakable for the remainder of each of their days.

"What did you decide to tell, well, *anyone*?" Opal finally asked.

"See? That's one of the odd things. The fire was just a smudge-pot in the morning, because most of the burnable stuff had been consumed by then. And no one, I mean no one, came by for almost a week," Hazel marveled.

"It was the weirdest thing, that's for sure," Travis agreed. "We went back to my little cabin in the daylight, and fell into a sleep that felt like death. Hazel on the bed, me in the chair first, then I ended up on the floor without knowing how I got there."

"When we woke up, I made some coffee and we sat on the back porch, just worrying what we'd say. We practiced a few different stories: Nathan went out preaching, my parents went to Santa Fe, stuff like that."

"In the end, we didn't really ever have to explain it to anyone. It was either no one knew us all together, or no one cared who lived there," Travis finally said.

Claire looked up quickly at her mother when Travis said that. Opal shook her head side to side, once and in a small, furtive gesture. Claire made a pleading look with her eyes. Opal narrowed her own. One more shake no.

"What are you two not saying, Opal?" said Shelly.

"Nothing. Now is not the time. It's nothing," Opal said, looking at Claire for acquiescence.

"Hmm. Ok, if you say so," Shelly said.

"I say so."

"So, then, what did you do about the property and ownership and taxes and all that legal stuff? I mean, surely someone had to have come around and made a stop?" Shelly turned to Hazel to ask this.

"Yes, well, that did finally happen. I think it was the next spring, but I really don't remember. They asked us— they being some guy in an old pickup—if James Gladstone ever intended to pay the taxes on the land. Travis looked like an adult by then. I didn't. But I was old enough to look like I belonged there, I guess. Travis asked if they could just tell him what the damages were and maybe he could pay them right then and there. I wandered off, but it must've worked out ok?" Hazel said.

"Hell, my knees were shaking right then! I had no idea if I could fake them out or not! But, they didn't seem to really want to know anything except where their money was. So they gave me the letter they were going to give James, which basically said he had 60 days to pay up or get chased off."

Chapter 51

Hazel serves pie

Hazel recalled the conversation with Luís, the one where he said her purpose was saving people at Gladstone, in startling clarity as she sat at the supper table. She yearned for the youth of that day when she sat with Luís and enjoyed his company and the day. Her aching bones hadn't arrived at that point, or else she was sure she would have sat just a few minutes longer each time they went into town.

Rousing herself from her after-supper stupor, she said, "I've got some pie. You all stay here while I get it. I remembered something that I want to tell you."

Shelly half-rose to help, then reconsidered and sat herself back down. She shared a rueful grin with Claire, who seemed content to keep pushing the salt and pepper shakers around in circles, chasing each other.

Hazel set a thick apple pie down in the center of the table, turned to get plates and forks, and then sat herself back down. The pie had a latticed top to the crust, and the apples had caramelized sugar oozing out of the gaps, crusted just right. It looked like the edges of a lava flow, where heat meets cool and solidifies into improbable, brittle shapes.

"I remembered something. A conversation."

Travis, the only one brave enough to encourage Hazel to keep the story moving, made a twirling motion with his right hand, which was propped on the back of his chair. He smiled at Hazel, though, so she knew he wasn't being impatient but more in the vein of supportive.

Hazel laughed. "Yeah, I did start this, didn't I? Here's what I wanted to tell you girls. All three of you."

They looked at her expectantly, and Claire stopped pushing the salt shaker through the beach of salt she had deliberately spilled out on the table. Hazel looked a second time at the salt spill, flickers of conflict passing as shadow on her face.

"Don't worry, Miss Hazel, I'll be sure to clean it up," Claire said.

"Oh, that's fine, sweetheart. It makes me of a mind to back when we had to be careful about using salt. It got so we'd scrape the extra salt off the hams and keep it in a jar to put into soup stock. That's been a while ago, hasn't it, Travis?"

"Sure has, Hazel. Now, why don't you tell us what's on your mind? You said you remembered something?"

"Yes. This will take a while to thread together, so, if I may be so forward, just let me ramble for a minute to get out all the pieces of cloth before I quilt them together for you, ok?"

They all nodded, intrigued at the prospect of a long story from Hazel, a rarity.

"Way back when, when Nathan was still alive, he'd always say, 'This place is sacred ground and it has a purpose for us.' He'd say it like it was a capital letter, or a cause, or like the way he'd read stories out of the Old Testament. I got good and sick of him talking like that, especially because he usually followed that statement up with a big old list of work that I was 'just the right person to do.'"

"I surely do remember him saying that! He'd take turns putting us to work, wouldn't he?" Travis chuckled.

"That was when he was still clear in his mind, even if he believed every single thing was related to how the Lord— the Lord Almighty—wanted him to live," Hazel said. "Anyway, we've exhausted that sickness of his—right into why he died that night. What I want you to think of is that he was the first one, of us, anyway, to say there was a purpose to this place.

"The second thing I want you to hear is that my mother truly believed this would be a good place. Even when she was trying not to sob, she still believed in better days.

I didn't know that then but after all these years of thinking on it, I do see it. She came out here with father on a quest. Thwarted, in the end, but still with a purity of intention that is rare. I owe her that remembrance."

Hazel sipped her tea, then dipped the spoon into the cup, swirled it slowly back and forth while she was lost in thought. Claire had a hot chocolate mustache, and she cheerily cleaned her upper lip with her tongue while her eyes smiled at Hazel. Shelly's head drooped in exhaustion. Opal sat stoically, waiting for yet another axe to fall.

"Should we finish all this tomorrow, ya think?" Travis asked, noticing that Shelly needed rest. "Shelly, you're asleep at the table—you must be tuckered out."

Shelly's eyes snapped open, and her mouth formed a small 'o'.

"No, no, I'm fine! Just wandered there for a minute. Don't you dare quit now! I'll hang in there. We all need to hear this."

"Ok, then. Here's the part that I remembered. Travis and I used to drive into Springer, and we'd get gas at the same station every time. That place is still there, but it's not the same family that used to own it. A Pueblo couple used to own it, and they brought her father along with them. It seemed like his only job was to sit in the sun on the bench and talk to the people who drove through. His name was Luís. I think we were both in our 20s when he was there and we talked the most. He's probably long gone now.

"Anyway, what he said, and we still don't know how he knew this, was that there 'was a purpose to our project'— and he would always twitch his fingers when he said 'project'—and we needed 'to stick with it for the good of those who would come along later.'"

At this, Opal and Shelly started slowly nodding their heads. A twinkle in Travis's eye, and Hazel continued to drive the point home.

"Yes, you see? All these years, and all that time we kept the secrets from you—out of shame, mostly—but more out of fear that you would leave. Because we, Travis and I, knew deep down, even if we'd forgotten, *that you three are the reason for this place.* If not for you, then why keep trying? If you three leave, then what happens to this place?"

Hazel shuddered to a stop, expelling a held breath and drawing in a full, shaky helping of fresh air. Claire could smell her exhale from across the table; a mouthful of old teeth, barely staving off the rot of poor or non-existent dental hygiene in the truly elderly. Claire, of course, had seen Hazel's near future when she napped in the young sprite hovering above the sleeping Hazel. Claire didn't say anything about any of that. She knew well enough that all Hazel needed was peace and love and care to ease her imminent passing.

Opal noticed the waft of decay, too, and laid her hand gently on Claire's arm. This common signal between them was rarely noticed by the others. It wasn't telepathy. Not really. Just a common ability to tap into a plane that stayed hidden from most others.

"We two will never leave. I've said it several different ways, but that is as declarative as I can make it. You two gave us a home. We have no other. And we want no other. Thank you sounds idiotic, but that's the core of what we want to say to you both," Opal declared. "Shelly, of course, you have been a rock, too, for us. A bridge between them and us. I hope you stay, too."

Chapter 52

The Rending of the Five

Shelly, while listening to Opal, and noticing the bond of communication between mother and daughter, began weeping. Not sobs, not even any sound. But steady tears that raced to her chin, hesitated, then flung themselves down to the table or onto her skirt. Only Shelly could tell how wide the crack in her firmament had grown, as wide as that of the very first rain back at the start of the great flood of Noah's time.

"I'm going to need the night to think about all this," Shelly said. "This has changed everything I've ever fully or partially understood about the world. I don't even, can't even figure out, know how I feel."

She slid her chair back, stood unsteadily, and said, "Would you all excuse me? I'll see you in the morning."

"Good night, Shelly," Claire said clearly. The others murmured or sketched a soft wave at Shelly, but she saw none of it as she turned for her close bedroom, entered, and shut the door tightly.

"That's not a good sign," Opal muttered.

"No, it ain't," agreed Travis.

"Well, I don't blame her. We've lived a lie for as long as she's known us," Hazel admitted.

Claire looked at her mother, who flicked her head side to side quickly, once more deterring Claire's insight from being shared.

"I'm shot, too," Travis said. "I'm gonna head on over and get some shuteye. Just cuz we've started sharing stories all night don't mean there ain't a pile of the same chores to be done in the morning."

He scraped his chair back, used a hand to pat both Opal and Claire on the shoulder fondly, then looked at Hazel. "Sleep well, little niece. It's been a good day. And worth it, to tell all this—don't you doubt that tonight while you lay there not sleeping."

"Ok, Uncle Travis. I'll try not to."

Hazel's voice had lowered and thinned, utterly weary and barely capable of producing sound. She left the table and went straight to her bed, pulling the comforter down and climbing straight in, not bothering to shut the door.

"Come on, Claire, let's get these dishes washed up and put away. Then we better get some sleep, too."

"Ok, Mom."

Later, when it was just Opal and Claire, they lay in the bed they often shared, eyes wide open and faces questioning each other.

"Tell me, Claire. Tell me all of what you saw and all of what you didn't say—you're safe now."

"They are both gonna die. It feels like they needed to tell us those things as part of the secret. Like, if they told us the secrets they've been keeping, then they'll get way older really fast and then not be able to stay around."

"Like it will kill them?"

"No, not exactly. But like they couldn't die if they didn't tell the whole truth. More like that."

"Hmm. Well, I wonder why that is?"

"Also. Shelly is going to leave. I can feel it," Claire said sadly.

"You think so? But she's always said she has nowhere else to go?"

"Yeah, but she doesn't trust this place anymore. The bad voice scared her when we walked out there today."

"Did she hear it? I thought you said only you heard it?"

"She didn't hear it, but she felt it. And she could tell I was telling the truth. And then there was all the old wrecks out in the arroyo that she'd never seen before."

The night had snuck upon them all while they sat at the table. Usually tuned in carefully to the rhythm of the day, they had all sat in conversation while the world spun on without them. The cattle in the barn, the pigs in the stock-house, the chickens under the porch and around the house, all cared little that the humans who usually showed themselves didn't make an appearance that afternoon. The sun shone brightly, then slanted down as it arced towards the mountains on the horizon, then finally gave way to a gloaming that waited impatiently for the moon to take charge.

Chapter 53

Shelly decides

The moon swung above the Gladstone Project, noting the pure and restful sleep of Opal and Claire, the fitful, restless tossing and turning that both Travis and Hazel experienced in their own beds. The moon woke Shelly from her first sleep, after her initial bout of dark, depressing escape had released its hold on her. She looked out the window on the silvered scrub, the shadows of the junipers imitating beings with hands upheld, fingers splayed with emotion and feeling. She was too tired to actually rise and walk around outside, but she felt a need. The need was so foreign to her that she actually thought she was dreaming of a bizarre place where she never did stay in this one place for the majority of her life.

Shelly felt an urge to leave. *Get up and go*, spoken clearly in her mind. Written clearly on the blackboard of her school days. All this happened while she lay in her bed; nothing actually physically changed in her surroundings. But the odd day of Claire's prophesying, and the strange appearance of the old vehicles in the arroyo had jarred her subconscious more than she realized during her waking day. It had taken the sleep to show her what her subconscious had been trying to tell her all day; that her place was no longer here at the Gladstone Project. Not that her years here were a waste, but more that her time had reached fullness and completion. And, if she stayed, she'd waste away quickly. As if the nourishment to be had in Gladstone could no longer be digested by her system. As if it lacked one critical mineral that made absorption impossible. A starving woman at a table of food meant for a different species, perhaps.

For the first time in dozens of years, she thought back to what her house looked like, back in the heavily forested turnout at the edge of the small town her father had ejected her from. She dropped back into sleep, the smell of the front room of her parents' house rising in her memory, as if she had just opened the door on a hot summer day. The front door had been varnished long ago; she had never known it any other way. The door faced west, and there were no trees to block the sun from baking the door through the screen. The metal screen door, made of flimsy aluminum, had a solid lower part with cheap metal scrollwork along the top two-thirds of the door. It was meant to imitate the classy estates of Old England, or perhaps the postbellum homes of the South after Reconstruction. But on the edge of the Ozarks on a gravel road attached to a plain rectangular house with sagging rain gutters, it added to the blowzy, tired, pathetic look of the home. A home that only someone raised in poverty could love, or miss, or long for. It was this very home that rose in Shelly's mind as she lay half-awake. As if reaching a previously unknown toxicity of radiation, she realized she'd had enough of the wide open spaces of the high desert scrub. All things she had marveled at and embraced as she passed most of her adulthood at Gladstone.

Resolved, she shut her eyes with the final thought that she would pack a small suitcase of things that she may one day care more about and look back on fondly. That fondness seemed unlikely right now, because of her disgust at the lie she'd been caught up in. But, you never know, she thought. She was going home to find her parents, after all. And if *that* wasn't an unlikely happy ending, she'd be surprised. She did love the two old people, after all, and Opal and Claire had been nothing but loving and generous and affirming and life-giving to her. Nevertheless…

"I've had enough of this. I'm going home," she murmured with her last waking sentiment. Although the moon rose and shone through her window, filtered by the thin, charmless, hand-sewn curtains, it didn't wake or even enter her dreams. It merely passed the night away, slowly sliding across the heavens to make way for the sun which would bring so many changes.

Chapter 54

Travis feels freedom

After the 'revelation', Travis had sat down in one of his trusty rockers on the porch.

The whole day's weather contradicted his emotion and the import of the conversation at the table in a startling way. Just a hint of night breeze brushed the air clear and forced the gnats off into the low brush. He felt bathed in the sympathy of the earth, as if it knew he'd had all he could take for the next few minutes. His eyes had gotten even older on the walk over to his chair. He could barely see; his eyelids drooped and the under bags had swollen so he had little better than slits left. He still gazed south, towards all that unsullied scrub, wishing he was strong enough to just go walk. Walk and not stop until he was tired well into the moonlight. Build a small, pure fire to heat some coffee maybe. Tear at a strip or two of jerky. Watch the stars reveal themselves as introduction to the great moon reigning supreme over the night. Sleep wrapped tightly in an old, thick blanket and wake at the skittering of the mice in the pre-dawn. He didn't concern himself with the logistics of the plan. He merely pined for the youth and freedom and innocence that such a journey asked for; an innocence, for sure, that was long gone in his weary soul.

A sense of freedom overcame his entire being. A release of guilt, perhaps? A loosening of the noose he'd carried around his neck ever since he killed his brother. Confession removed it all.

Another set of tears reluctantly left the safety of his eyes and succumbed to gravity, detouring around each stalk of stubble on his cheeks. He cried for those simpler days, his brother (but there was really no other answer, not back then), his brother and his lovely sister-in-law (if there was one more he could have rescued that night, it would have been Lily), for poor Hazel. Hazel, he could tell that very night, was ruined forever as far as truly trusting outsiders would go. Her own uncle, driven to action by a misplaced zeal for a messiah (who would never dream of asking a penitent man for the kind of sacrifice he offered), slicing the heartstring that held her regard for humanity close to her own soul.

There was no one to absolve Travis from the reality that he was the youngest of three, and the responsibility for determining sanity and insanity should never have fallen to him. His parents, by sending them west, abdicated their own judgeship over their offspring, thus leaving Travis to clean up the mess. Of course, there was no one to tell Travis *this* either, so he became just as mentally crippled as he believed Hazel was.

It surely wasn't pure chance that first Shelly and then Opal and Claire felt a pull to stop at Gladstone, but not even a trained spiritualist, let alone a qualified psychiatrist, could point with any certainty to the support and peace and harmony those three women brought when they stayed.

A property, sometimes, knows what it needs and purposes itself to attract what it lacks. Many plants change their scent to better attract insects that then come and help with the pollination that ensures a species' survival across the years.

So who's to say the land couldn't press its case to prospective settlers?

Chapter 55

Travis

As he pushed the rocker with one heel in the dusk, his thoughts trailed backward in a sort of primal review. Travis now could see that adobe house as it truly was in those days, a crudely shaped, barely habitable sod hut with low ceilings. James had chopped a hole in the ceiling to run stove pipe through, but they'd gone almost a month with a hole there and no pipe to put into it. In truth, James hadn't even ordered the pipe for several weeks after he chopped the hole. Smoke from the stove eventually escaped out of the hole, but they all existed in a blue haze whenever they were inside.

Travis had refused to climb up on the shaky roof to try and make the hole.

"Get your lazy hide up there and dig a chimney hole out!" James'd said to Travis. Lily, useless and whining, wrung her hands and looked pained.

"Let me up there, James," she'd said, a clear look on her face that telegraphed that she hoped beyond hope that James would not let her.

"You're useless, Lily. You barely can cook, let alone do any work," he'd said bitterly.

Travis surprised himself that he remembered all this; he'd long thought they had the perfect relationship.

Travis roused himself at the thought that perhaps the James and Lily show was in dire straits and was about to crumble. Cry 'uncle' and retreat in one direction or another. Travis and Hazel back then had been far too young to see any of that at the time. He had another thought—was it possible that Nathan had seen the fracturing and didn't want the time at Gladstone to end? As Travis stitched together scraps of memory, he saw a way where it was actually Nathan, middle brother—younger than James and older than Travis—who had been trying to encourage James and Lily to continue on. And when Nathan saw it was fruitless, he had tried to remove James and Lily from the scene so he could carry on the mission of Gladstone with only Travis and Hazel to help him. That Travis had rebelled and stood up to Nathan when he saw the dead James and Lily had surely, sorely, surprised Nathan.

He'd risen to adulthood that day, he now realized, and the series of decisions he'd made after killing his own brother unspooled in front of him like a documentary. He rocked slightly in the chair, the only movement in that dark, mostly unused front room, a metronomic review of his many years on earth. He was tired. His chin drooped, his eyelids dropped to almost closed, and his feet finally stopped adding energy to the equation that kept the rocker in movement.

The rocker, with its lifelong companion aboard, finally stopped its perpetual motion. Travis, too, earthbound—oh, these many years—finally left his wrung-out human form and arose to share in the light breeze, tinged with sage, that skipped across the high desert scrub. Only the field mice that had taken up residence in the walls of the kitchen sensed that, though a human still remained, it was safe to claw up the curtains to the counter and see if a meal could be found for themselves and the new litter of kits that filled the nest in the wall.

Chapter 56

Hazel

Not knowing what anyone else on Gladstone was thinking or feeling, Hazel arose well before sunup and made her purpose one clear-headed walk out to the edge of the property. She'd told her entire story, the best she could, the night before, to the only people in the world who she knew and loved and cared for and trusted. In that she was content to let the chips fall where they may. Although she had promised Travis that she'd never reveal what happened the night of the fire, the grim reality that the girls knew far more than they should, and far more than they could let go, showed her that the only path forward was to come entirely clean about the history of how Travis and Hazel had come into possession of Gladstone.

She thought about the land transfer, then, while she shuffled out to the spring. It had been an easy afternoon of work with old paper, calligraphic pens, and some practiced signatures to show the line of land succession from the original cad named Harris to James and Lily Gladstone to joint ownership of Travis and Hazel Gladstone, co-owners of the

Gladstone Property. They already had the legal description of the boundaries from when James had purloined them from Harris's stuff. They merely wrote letters, dated suitably, that had stood up quite well in Clayton, the county seat at the time. Those clerks, she remembered, had little interest in some plot of land west of them by almost two hours that had little value to it except for an intermittent spring that used to be important.

She wore her mother's work boots; the ones she'd had ever since her mother had bought them down in Springer. They'd splurged on a fine luncheon at the Brown Hotel, then strolled the main street in the sun. Lily had urged her into the mercantile and then walked her over to the newly-arranged women's section, where there were a few dresses, a parasol, a few hats, and some boots. The boots were functional, yet they had a daring trim along and under the laces of red silk. Lily was quite taken with them and wanted to buy them both a pair, matching. She insisted that they'd "take one pair in the young girl's size," and "a pair that will fit me." Once Hazel outgrew her own boots, she wore her mother's boots, saved from the fire, only on special occasions.

Appropriate now, as she wore them out onto the road that led to the arroyo, feeling both an exhausting age which tugged her breath away, and also a youthful free exuberance, that, had she been truly younger, would have caused her to twirl in circles as she advanced down the road.

She whimsically scuffed the dirt in front of her, once with each toe, and watched the miniature dust cloud slide off the road and into the sage that lined the track. She set her eyes on the slight curve at the uppermost part of the track, which, once gained, led down to the edge of the arroyo. She now recalled that Claire had said something about a wagon? Or a car—surely not—that had shown itself revealed in the new scouring through the arroyo that the latest storm had brought? "I'd like to see that," she murmured to herself.

It was high time Claire took charge of the entirety of Gladstone, especially since Hazel could feel her matriarchy slipping away—giving way—to Opal and Shelly. Opal perhaps more than Shelly, she noticed, examining the dynamics of the situation around the dinner table the preceding night. She hoped that the short conversation she and Claire had about Gladstone would be enough for Claire to continue on with the work. The only work that mattered; saving lost souls.

Little wonder that Hazel no longer wielded the power she once had; the time when she had the energy to whittle away at every problem had long since passed. In truth, the expansion of the property to include the RV parking and the increased focus on the sales in the front mercantile had been the true exchange of power, though she was just realizing it now. She made a note to ask Travis if he had realized they were no longer in charge of their own home. Surely he had noticed, although she conceded that he may simply not care enough to do anything to forestall it.

Her lungs continued to make heavy work of the simple act of pulling in and pushing out air. Possible that she hadn't walked like this in a long time, but it didn't feel normal to her. She stopped, halfway up the rise, the short, steepest section left to climb until the arroyo was in view. She put her hands on her hips, and stepped a slow circle to see the entire circumference of her view. The hazy mountains sketched a horizon off to the west, made blue by the impending sunrise, and the first threads of gold had crested the flat eastern horizon. Her spirit felt light, yet her body felt wrung out. Her chest hurt; the thudding of her heart pushing her ribcage to its limit. Can one's heart break a rib if it beats too hard, she idly wondered.

Feeling little relief, she quelled her misgivings along with an urge to turn back to the Gladstone house, and walked up the right half of the twin tracks separated by the thin cheatgrass that lined the center of the road. She topped the rise, still out of breath, and continued along the slight downhill to near the arroyo, where a trail led off to the left. The trail led to the origin of this arm of the arroyo that always had a trickle of water even in the driest of times. The head of the arroyo, a tiny box canyon, far too small to be used as an actual corral for livestock, which is where the term came from, had several different sections of the vertical, stratified clay. Seeps from the spring darkened the earth and puddled at the base of the wall, a mere six feet tall, and formed a mossy pool a foot or two across. She sat gratefully on the light sandstone rock that sat at the edge of the pool.

It was cold in the shade of the spring's wall, formed by who knows what initial water that began the arroyo way back when. The spring, always present and never explained, continued to trickle its pure water down the sidewall, into the pool, and the slow dribble lazed past Hazel's feet as she stared into the moss. So tired, she thought. She thought perhaps if she could just stretch her legs out she could catch her breath and her head would stop hurting so badly.

She slid down the smooth sandstone until her back was against the stone, her butt was in the dry dirt at its base, and her feet stretched out almost to the edge of the pool. Her left boot, closer to the pool, actually sat in the edge of the water. Her skirt began to slowly soak up water while she sat there. Hazel had closed her eyes, and her mind had detached from a true consciousness. The sun still sat below the edge of the spring's wall, but daylight had arrived. A dragonfly hovered above the water, flitting in to sip, then retreating to the shadow, ever on guard for the swallows that lived in holes along the arroyo. A coyote trotted towards the pool, stopped when it smelled the uncommon, but not unknown, scent of a human. The human form slumped against the rock, unmoving. The coyote approached slowly, so slowly. An atavistic sense pulled the animal to the water because of the need, even as the instinct kept every muscle tensed for flight.

No movement would come from the dignified old woman, who had peacefully slipped away into her dreams and then into death with nary a whisper of protest. The coyote lapped at the water, first quietly, as a predator, then thirstily, as it became clear that he was the master of the watering hole at this moment in time. Sated, he trotted up to the woman, sniffed the death, and, perhaps in leaner times, the possibility of meat, that sat for the taking, yet moved on into the morning sun and along his way.

Chapter 57

Shelly leaves

Shelly's window had full sun in it before she raised her eyelids and roused herself from an untroubled sleep. She fully remembered her thoughts of home from the night before. And she fully remembered when they slipped into her dreams. In her dream, she had opened the door of her house, the door that smelled of the sun-scorched varnish, and laid her eyes upon her smiling parents, both standing, both open-armed, welcoming her home. She had little doubt that her homecoming would be entirely joyous, but her heart almost burst at the thought of at least trying. So many years had passed, an equal number for all of them, that it was folly to think they would still be angry that she'd left them like she did. A small weasel of hope emerged from hiding in her subconscious that, when she showed her face at home, her parents would cry with relief that someone was there to care for them and provide for them, and that they could finally rest. She nursed that small coal of hope while she lay in her bed, all while thinking about the practicalities of her egress from the Gladstone Project.

She swung her legs out of bed energetically, flicked the quilt carelessly back into place, not bothering to straighten the pillows or the sheets to match or square. "I'm done with that," she said to herself. It was a freeing declaration; one that she wished she didn't have to worry about, but was always too needful of the approbation of at least Hazel, and maybe Travis, though he rarely stuck his head into any of the bedrooms in the main house. "Today is the day I return to myself. Today I quit running and hiding from myself," she said.

Like many paradigm-shattering decisions, this one came quietly but firmly from a woman who'd barely left this patch of land for years and years and years. Of course, she'd gone into town now and then, but never with a sense of adventure or purpose in pursuit of anything grander than a supply list. She stood in the sun of her window, assessing what she'd take, what she'd leave, and whether she'd say anything to anyone of the other four about her leave-taking. She dressed quickly and simply, wearing trousers for a change, because she thought that might be easier to travel through bus stations, or cities, or hitch rides in. She really wasn't sure what clothing would make her look the most assured, but she figured pants, boots, and her light jean jacket would be unremarkable and also useful through any weather changes.

She pulled her heavy canvas bag down from her closet. It had a drawstring at the top, and a single strap to carry it either over her shoulder or cross-body if one preferred. She filled it about half-full with clothing and a few toiletries. As she entered the kitchen, she set the bag down in a chair at the table. The dishes from the night before had been washed and neatly stacked to the left of the sink. There was no coffee made, nor any breakfast items out or dirty dishes from earlier breakfasts. It was unusual that Hazel hadn't been up before her for coffee and breakfast, but not unprecedented. She thought little of it while she sliced herself a few pieces of bread and put them in wax paper to take with her.

Her plan had coalesced in her mind as she packed to get out to the road in time to flag the early bus that ran eastward twice a week—one of the days, Tuesday, happened to be today. If she scooted, she could be out on the bench and waiting to climb aboard. Several years ago, when a couple's car had broken down and they needed to get back east, they built a tall stanchion at the far west part of their property that ran along the edge of the road. They had a flag which they could raise which was bright red and had the words "STOP, Please" stitched on it.

Shelly walked out the front of the house, trotted to the stanchion and raised the flag, then stepped quickly back to the bench under the cottonwood to wait and see if she'd beaten the bus. Ten minutes later, she heard the downshifting of the bus coming around the slight bend. She stood quickly, hoisted her bag, and walked to the edge of the gravel in line with the bench. The bus slowed, a rush of air coming with it, the wake of a heavy land-ship wafting over her.

The door of the bus swung open with a hiss of compressed air, and the bus lowered itself almost to the ground, making it easier to step aboard. Shelly turned one last time to look at Gladstone, her left foot already aboard, for a last look at her 'home no longer'. She didn't notice young Claire watching her through the curtains, which was probably a mercy, because the pain of whether to stay or go would have been amplified by her decision to say goodbye, or apologize, or declare love and sadness and joy all at once.

"Hello, there, ma'am, looks like you need a ride," a cheery voice greeted her.

She looked up into the plump, shiny face of a man in uniform.

"I surely could. May I buy a ticket to Joplin, Missouri?" she asked.

"Oh, well, why don't you just ride along until we get to Clayton, and you can settle up with the ticket box there. How does that sound?"

"That sounds just fine, thank you," she said gratefully.

She stepped along the aisle of the half-full bus, and picked a seat on the road side, so she wouldn't have to force herself to not look at Gladstone as she pulled away.

Chapter 58

Shelly and the Ozarks

Shelly's remaining story is simply told, at least in as much as it pertains to her decision to leave Gladstone and seek peace with her family back east. She did indeed stop in Clayton to buy a ticket back to Joplin, and realized that the bus would get there in the midnight hours of the very same day she left Gladstone. Not wanting to lower the odds of a happy homecoming by arriving well after what she was sure was bedtime, she asked if she could change her ticket to stop somewhere along the way to wait for a bus that drove through Joplin closer to supper time. The option of stopping in Leon, Kansas, this evening, and then picking up the morning bus that left out of Wichita destined for a four p.m. stop in Joplin seemed like it would work just fine.

"There's usually space in the B&B right next to the post office in Leon if you want," the ticket agent had said.

"I'd like that," she'd replied.

"I'll give them a call when you all move on; let them know you'd like a room," he'd said back.

A simple thank you from her and the transaction was made.

The bus left after a short delay for all the various travel transactions that always had to take place, and she took nearly the same seat she'd started in. It was a good seven-hour stretch, not counting the stops in all the small towns along the way. This bus driver hated to have people use the toilet in the back, because it quickly made the recirculated air less than fresh, which made riders tetchy, and he didn't need any more bad reviews along his route. So he'd stop almost every two hours, which stretched the seven-hour trip into almost nine. The burg of Leon arrived in due course, Shelly dismounted with her one canvas bag, and saw that the bus stop was the post office, and there was little else along the highway between the two signs that marked the township of Leon. She walked up the steps of the B&B called The Haven of Leon—"come stay a while" on a nicely painted wooden sign out front. The door opened as she mounted the last step.

"You must be the lady who'd like a place to stay?" said a smiling gentlewoman.

"I am indeed. Shelly is my name. Many thanks," she added.

The stay, while comfortable, was unremarkable. In the morning, she sat ready in the rocker on the porch of The Haven of Leon, awaiting the bus. She remarked on the humidity which had drawn a sweat along most of her back, her forearms, her hairline.

"Oh, you just wait until it heats up. This is nothing."

She got on the bus, her stomach finally fluttering at what she was about to attempt as she got to Joplin. This stretch of road was uneventful, and she dozed her way along until the flat plains started to give way to the wooded and hilly markers that indicated the huge tracts of Ozark forest were not far away. In Joplin, she left the bus, found a taxi, and asked it to take her to the southeast part of town. When they got there, they drove from the stately and well-kept homes and into the smaller, plainer, messier ones that she remembered. They traveled out of that area into an area that she now would call seedy and long past a repairable reputation. She asked the driver to drop her at an intersection about two blocks from her house; she didn't want a way to chicken out after coming this far.

"You sure, ma'am? This ain't the best part of town anymore," he'd said.

"Yes, yes, I'll be fine," she said, a trifle impatiently. "I'm from here."

"If you say so. But not many people claim to be from here anymore, just so you know."

"I understand," she said, handing him cash. "Please keep the change; I appreciate the ride."

Hitching her bag over one shoulder, she walked—if not boldly, then resolutely—towards the house of her childhood, one block down and one block over. A dog on a chain barked at her on the other side of a rusty chain-link fence, the yard entirely dirt from the animal's frenetic running. As she turned the corner to her street, a wave of emotion stopped her dead in her tracks. A young child on a bicycle wove her way unsteadily down the street towards her. The girl saw an old woman just standing there, and as the girl got closer, she noticed the lady was trembling.

"You ok, lady?" she said, not unkindly.

"Ah. Yes. I believe so," Shelly said. "Although could you tell me who lives in that house right there?"

Shelly had pointed to a rundown, single-level house with a tiny porch edged with a cheap black metal low railing. The blinds were all down. One downspout hung at an angle, barely attached to the gutter. The other downspout at the far end of the house lay on the ground, right next to the broken asphalt driveway that had been almost fully subsumed by crabgrass. The yard hadn't been mowed for a long time, if at all. What wasn't weeds was tall and undisciplined buffalo grass. The screen door hung open. A red square sticker was in the middle of the old wooden door, but it was too far away for Shelly to be able to read what it said.

"*Nobody* lives there, lady. Can't you tell?" the little girl said scornfully.

"Since when?" Shelly finally asked.

"Them two old people hated all of us. They died a while ago. Her first, then him right after her."

"Really? Both of them are dead?"

"Yup. Fine with me. All he ever did was yell at me to get out of his driveway."

A screen door banged from a house right close by, and a woman came out on the step.

"Lauren? Who are you talking to?" the lady said loudly once she saw Shelly talking to the girl on the bike.

"This lady here was walking right down the middle of the street, Mom. I was just—"

"Hello, ma'am. Are you ok? Can I help you with something? We certainly aren't buying, if you're selling," she said.

"Oh, no. It's just—I used to live in that house. I was just asking this nice young lady if she knew who lived there."

"Ah. Well, you're in luck. They already died and took their misery with them. I'll tell you what, there wasn't one person who ever tried to talk to them or help them that ever got anywhere with them. They were just plain mis—" She stopped as she noticed Shelly's eyes had filled with tears.

"Those two sure sound like my parents," she finally said. "I had hoped to come home and—"

"Oh, honey. I'm so sorry," the mother said, with feeling. She approached Shelly, rubbed one shoulder. "But let me tell you, unless I'm off my rocker, that reunion would have been the shortest on record."

"They kicked me out as a teenager. I've never come home. I've been waiting all this time for them to figure out they were wrong."

"I'm so sorry. But, I'm tellin' ya, you're better off this way."

Shelly stood in confusion for a long while, then walked with the nice mother who had tugged gently on her jean jacket sleeve to get her to come onto their porch and out of the street. She sat on the metal glider, sipping on the proffered cup of coffee, lost in thought. Wondering what the next chapter would be now that she had left the only other home she'd known.

Chapter 59

Opal and Claire remain

The fateful day when Travis and Hazel both died, and Shelly left without knowing about either death or saying goodbye, Opal and Claire had awoken early. They quietly agreed to stay in bed and wait for the warmth of the sun to fill the room before they went out to see how much of their world had changed. Opal, because she didn't want to talk about the history anymore, and Claire because she knew all too well that her predictions would be true. Their tiny world of Gladstone, where five people lived and loved each other, would be forever changed. Claire didn't necessarily think that was a bad thing, but she knew that it would be sad and unfixable. They both heard the front door open when Shelly stepped outside, and they heard the bus grind to a stop. Claire had gotten out of bed and watched through the curtains when Shelly got on the bus. Claire decided not to go out on the porch to wave. There was no point, was there?

By the time Opal and Claire had eaten breakfast, made some hot cocoa—which they both preferred over the bitter, stove-top coffee—and gotten dressed, it was mid-morning.

Opal had asked Claire to go with her to make sure that Travis had taken care of the livestock. She also had a small, nagging worry that they hadn't seen Hazel yet that day. Even if she left the house in the early morning, she would usually return in pretty good time for another cup of coffee or some toast.

As they walked towards the barn, they heard the lowing of the milk cows that had a strained, desperate note in them. She opened the barn and saw that none of them had been milked early as they were accustomed to, and their bags had filled beyond the comfortable. Opal quickly got them lined up, hooked them up to the milking machines, and then turned them back out into the near pasture by opening the barn door on the far side of the farmyard. They'd hurried to check the hogs, too.

The pigs were merely irritated and hungry, so when Opal and Claire swung the doors open, the pigs greeted them with squeals which meant joy, not pain. Once the two had shut the doors of the pig barn, they had looked at each other and wondered where everyone had gone. Claire pointed at the boot prints in the dust of the arroyo road. A very small boot, with very worn tread, had walked along the road, over-stepping the windswept miniature sand dunes that always formed. There was no returning set of tiny boot prints, al-though a larger set in the other track probably belonged to

Shelly from when Shelly and Claire had walked out and back the day before. They turned for the arroyo, wondering what they would find of Hazel when they got there.

As they reached the end of the road, which dove down into the arroyo itself and had a ghost of a road back up the other side, they saw that no tracks led down into or back out of the arroyo. Retracing a dozen yards, they took the small trail that led to the spring. At the spring, they found Hazel, peaceful in death, reclined against a rock, her feet and skirt wet from the soaking of the pool. They left her there so they could go back and get the truck—as light as she was, she was far too heavy to carry all that way back to Gladstone House.

And, of course, when they went into Travis's house to check on him and see why he hadn't cared for the cows or pigs, they came upon his own peaceful death scene. Opal merely looked at Claire, who shrugged her shoulders, and then they hugged each other tightly.

The details of the burials, the mourning, and the land transfers took place much as lava flows form a fresh crack, or as water forms a new channel for a long-running river. Slowly, but predictably, they got the two old people buried, out by the graves of James and Lily, with simple wooden crosses to mark the passing of the two people who, arguably, saved them from destruction those years ago. Travis and Hazel had indeed written a will that gave joint ownership of the entirety of the Gladstone Property to Opal, Claire, and Shelly. Once again, the blasé county assessor's office took the information in stride, and dutifully changed the names on the deed to reflect that two of the three designees had accepted their part ownership in the property, and the third person was currently being searched for. If, in fact, Shelly could be found, they would add her signature to the documents that gave full ownership, property rights excluding mineral rights (as was standard), and taxation to the three women listed in the will.

It would have been problematic had Claire been the only one to lay claim to the property because she was a minor. But since her own mother was also a beneficiary, the succession was fairly straightforward.

Chapter 60

Opal and Claire

Opal sucked her finger while sitting at the kitchen table. She'd seen the glint in Claire's eye when they got the ownership papers, and it swept her right back to the day she left Taos.

She was lucky to have gotten out alive with the baby. That man had killing on his mind, and he would not be stopped by pretty words, or diversions of the skin, or food, or drink. He'd laid the machete down for a second while he went out back to get another six-pack from the garage, and she grabbed the baby and ran for dear life. She had no idea what he did when he came back in. All she knew was that he didn't come after her, or if he did, he didn't find them. Mercifully, an old rancher with a battered straw cowboy hat had stopped to let her in and give her a ride to the bus station on the east side of town. She bought a ticket on the eastbound bus—no charge for an infant—sat in terror while it idled for another 30 minutes, then shook again with fear every time the bus stopped on the way past Eagle's Nest, Cimarron, and Springer. Past Cimarron, but before Springer, she looked out the bus window to see a truck careening past them on a long straightaway, lights flashing and horn honking. It turned out to be some random driver, but it scared her even harder than she was already. She finally stepped off the bus at Gladstone, those many years ago, because she couldn't stand one more stop where he might catch up with them.

Opal sat and thought about that same glint in two sets of eyes—three sets of eyes, really. The first set, way back when she was a child, out in the hills around Taos. She'd seen a mountain lion. She had to go back home and ask her father what animal it was she actually saw, by describing its behavior.

"It looked like a huge cat, Dad. But crouched and ready to jump."

"You don't know how close you came to being dead, then, Opal," her dad had said.

The cat, a tawny, dusty gold, had glared at her with its head lowered almost to its carefully placed front paws. The cat's back legs had disappeared under the body of the animal, but there was a ferocious energy, crackling off the hair on its spine, like static electricity surging to close a circuit. Opal stopped walking. She dropped the two rocks she was carrying in her one hand, small ones that she had collected to take home. The rocks had lines running through them, layers of different colors. The rocks reminded her of that fancy cake they sometimes got to eat when they went to the cafe. Something about three milks.

The animal, through the force of its will, held Opal's gaze and she simply couldn't look away. She actually remembered when she tried to turn her neck. It creaked upon starting, then immediately froze in place like a rusted hinge. The arc of Opal's life changed in that moment, though it would take all these years to realize it. That hypnotic, magnetic, pitiless gaze, from a mountain lion in the Rockies, taught her how small and helpless she was and always would be. She lived or died at the pleasure, no—at the *whim*, of a predator. Had the predator not just filled its rough tongue with the blood of a desert hare Opal would have understood the Great Circle of Life. As it was, she was introduced to a master class in fear. The lifetime it took for Opal to take steps backwards along the thin game trail until the cat looked back down to its few remaining bits of bloody fur took only minutes. As if scientific chronology had any sway over her universe at that moment. Had she been a poet, she would have, after this incident, been able to describe the passing seasons, the cycle of life, death, rebirth. But especially death, or at least the threat of death.

As Opal, sitting on the hard metal seat of the ancient tractor, drove back to the farmyard, those eyes of the mountain lion roared back into her consciousness because she had seen the exact same look in both her boyfriend's eyes, and then in Claire's eyes, who was indeed the scion—or was it spawn?—of that same boyfriend. Never in Opal's life did she think she would have to re-open the chapter of ugliness that filled her time with that man. He had a name. She refused to use it, and dearly hoped that he had already succumbed to some unnamed, incurable, wasting disease that left him alive but mocked his humanity by turning him into a shell that could do nothing for itself. She parked the tractor, stepped down into the dirt, and went to find Claire. They had to talk.

Claire, of course, had no idea who or where her father was. Her mother steadfastly refused to talk about any life before Gladstone. She was curious, but not obsessively so, and when her mother continually changed the subject, Claire moved on. Upon realizing they were solely in charge of Gladstone, though (unless Shelly came back), Claire wondered if she could arrange to get her birth father to come visit, maybe stay, maybe join their life.

"I'll start here. Maybe someday we can go find him," she said, surprised at herself.

Chapter 61

Opal and Claire
ask for help

"Mom, it's time," Claire said later that day.

"Taos, do you mean?" Opal said.

"I do."

"You're right. We need to go back. I don't want to, but we better go make sure we can close the door and keep it closed."

"Or… maybe my dad wants to come back with us," Claire said.

Opal didn't say anything. Just reached her arm across the old, scratched table, bunching the lace tablecloth a little, and held her daughter's hand.

"I guess anything's possible."

They made preparations for a day, puzzling over what to do with the milk cows; after all, they couldn't just put production on hold while the girls quested after answers. Eventually, they decided to call the assessor and ask him for help.

"Mr. Glen? This is Opal, from out at the Gladstone Project. Do you remember helping us a little while back?" Opal said.

A pause while she listened.

"Yes, that's us. No, we haven't really gotten the project off the ground. You were right, it's taking a lot more work than any of us thought. Plus… well, it's just the two of us now."

Listening.

"Yes, just me and Claire, my daughter. Shelly went back home. Hazel and Travis have passed."

Silence.

"Well, thank you, we appreciate that. Well, you couldn't have known. We didn't call anyone. Anyway, the reason we are calling is that we need some help with the livestock for a few days. We were wondering if you knew anyone who could tend the milk cows and the pigs."

Opal switched the phone to the other hand while he talked.

"Well, that'd be great. Yes, I'll wait for a call from him. Snell, you say? And yes, we'd pay him. We don't have much, but it'd be three days, maybe four, of milking. Plus feeding hogs."

A last pause.

"Thanks so much, Mr. Glen. We've got to go back to Taos and figure some stuff out. Ok, you have a good day. Thanks," Opal finished, setting the handset back in the cradle.

Claire looked up at her, questioning.

"Yeah, he'll help us out. He's got a guy named Mr. Snell who will call later today and get the details. I think we can leave tomorrow morning after we milk. What do you say to that?" Opal asked.

"That sounds ok. And, Mom?"

"Yes?"

"This is the right thing. We have to go find my dad, even if you're scared."

"You'd be scared, too, if you knew him, Claire," Opal said wearily.

Chapter 62

Opal, Claire, and Taos

After the milking, then, they each put a bag in the back of the old farm pickup, hopped into the cab, and headed west. They drove to Springer, where they gassed up, then headed west through the heart of the New Mexican Rockies until they got to the wide valley that cradled the Rio Grande. Opal slowed as she entered the city limits, looking left and right at the first major three-way stop. She continued west, then turned south. When they got to a section of official, but humble, buildings, she waved her hand towards one building in particular.

"That's the place your dad told me he was going to take you," Opal said.

"But you didn't let him, did you?"

"Nope. That's when I ran and left with you. We lived down this way. I'm headed that way to see if it looks like they are still there."

"Ok. It's gonna be ok, Mama."

"I doubt it. But we've come this far, so…"

Opal took another turn or two, heading generally south for less than a mile. She pulled off the road into a graveled parking lot.

"Right down there."

Claire looked that way, then looked at her mother.

"Looks like this gym and the Dollar General are new. But see that old, ratty fence? With the buildings behind it? That's it."

Claire reached out to hold her hand.

"Let's go check it out, Mama."

Opal took her foot off the brake, eased forward, coasting to a stop in front of the closed farm gate in the piñon-staved fencing.

"That old truck looks the same. It's the same trailer. Painting still hasn't been finished. I think it's the same family," Opal said.

Opal got out to see if the gate was locked or just chained. She lifted the loop of rusted wire holding it closed, swung it open so she could pull the truck through. As the gate stopped its opening arc, a dog roused off the porch and stalked towards them. Opal trotted back to the pickup, swung herself in, and shut the door quickly.

"Is your window closed, Claire?"

"No. It's hot."

"Close it! Quickly. I don't trust that dog."

Sure enough, the dog circled the truck, snarling, and then jumped at the window even as Claire cranked the handle as fast as she could. Opal drove into the yard, leaving the truck running, facing the sagging wooden porch that sat beneath the main door of the half-painted trailer. She honked the horn. Waited.

An old woman in a loose house dress opened the door, leaning on the doorknob to support herself. She put her free hand above her eyes to shield the sun and get a better look into the truck. She turned her head and spoke something into the house. Turned back to face the truck. Shuffled two steps forward to lean on the porch railing. The railing sagged outward. The woman snarled at the dog. The dog stopped its own snarling, and slunk under the trailer.

"Who are you and what do you want? This is private property," the woman said.

She said it mildly, but Opal could tell she'd been saying it for years in the same way, in the same situations. Different truck, maybe—merely a new verse to the same tired song.

Opal lowered her window, checked for the dog, stuck her head out.

"Hello, Mrs. Medina. It's Opal," she said simply.

The woman turned back to the house and shouted inside, "Davis! Come out here!"

Opal turned to Claire. "That's your grandma. She just hollered for your dad."

Claire sat straight up, wide-eyed, absorbing.

During the impasse, in which Opal stared at Mrs. Medina and Mrs. Medina looked back at Opal's worried face hanging out of the truck, Claire inched to the middle of the bench, sitting hip to hip with her mother and putting her hand on Opal's leg.

A scraggly man stepped out of the truck onto the porch. He didn't have a shirt on, and his long hair shone with grease. The body kind, not the hair salon kind. He had tattoos on both shoulders, plus a stylized cross on his chest right in the middle. His jeans were greasy, too, and hung on his hip bones like they'd been hung in a closet on pegs. No shoes. Copper bangles on each wrist.

"Well, I'll be damned, it's my girl Opal," he said, baring his teeth. Maybe a smile, maybe a snarl—too soon to tell.

"Who's that you got with you?" the mother said.

"This is Claire," Opal said.

"Is that the kid?" Davis asked.

Opal nodded, said nothing.

"You two may as well come in," the mother said. "I'll make somethin' to eat and drink."

She turned from the porch rail, went back inside, shifting her grip from rail to knob to inside furniture to aid her pained shuffling. Opal didn't move; she just sat there, looking at Davis.

"You'll be safe. I ain't got no energy to do nothin'," Davis said. "Mother's right; come on in."

He motioned with his hand, turning to go back inside, too. He turned back.

"Don't worry about the dog none. He's all bark but is useless when the chips are down."

Opal and Claire, sharing a look, finally stepped down from the cab, into the dust, and walked toward the steps. When they mounted them, the whole porch trembled. It held their weight, though, and they stepped across the threshold of the mobile home. Body odor washed out the door, overlaid with both old and new skillet grease, and punctuated with perking coffee.

Leaning up to her mother's ear, Claire said, "She's awfully sick already, Mama. Go easy, ok?"

Not surprised at Claire's comment, Opal looked at her with a half-smile, nodding her head.

"She's not our problem, I don't think."

Chapter 63

Opal, Claire, and Taos

Davis had set himself back in the corner of the main room of the home, slumped in a tired recliner covered in pilled fabric that had more stains than original color. He had a tall Bud Light can in his hand, emptying it as they stepped in.

"I never did get around to figuring out why you left, did I?" he said.

"You knew danged well why she left, Davis. You're dangerous is why," Mrs. Medina said from the kitchen. The kitchen was only two steps to the left of the door. She stood over a cast iron skillet that popped with both bacon and rellenos that looked as if they'd been sitting in that skillet for a day or two.

"You two hungry?" she asked. "We were just about to have some lunch. I can throw a few extra in here if you want."

"No thanks. We got a burger up at Blake's before we came down here."

"Whoa. Rich now, are you?" Davis said.

Opal took a deep breath, wishing she had a way to run the conversation the way she'd envisioned it. In the end, it was Claire who took charge.

"You're my daddy, aren't you?" she asked.

Davis, who'd been reaching for another beer from the cooler next to him, stopped his arm and sat up straight. He looked at the girl.

"I ain't got no earthly idea if I'm your daddy. D'you know why?" he asked, his voice rising at the end.

"Because Mama left before you could give me away."

"I wasn't givin' no kid away. Where'd you hear that?"

"It's the truth, right?" Claire said.

"I ain't gonna take no sass from some kid who says she's my kid. Not when an old flame who ran out on me is standin' here asking me for money. I've heard enough. How about you two git on—"

"Davis, it's time you shut your mouth and listened for a minute," Opal said.

He opened his mouth to start in again, and Opal put her hand out like a traffic cop, palm facing him.

"Stop. Just stop. Let me say what I came to say, and then we'll be on our way," Opal insisted, a power coming into her that flowed from Claire's bravery.

"Let her say her piece, Davis," agreed Mrs. Medina.

Opal cast a grateful look to her before turning back to Davis. She breathed.

"What you did to me the day I left was against the law. What you said to me about taking the baby to the agency was cruel. At the time, I had to believe you meant it. There was no way that you were taking my little one from me, and it made several things come clear."

He started to talk, and Opal raised her hand again.

"You hear me out. I'll tell you when I'm done."

That old fury had crept into his brow, but he stayed seated and Opal took this ill grace as permission to continue. The popping from the skillet had stopped and had been replaced by a cupboard door banging, a plate set down on the counter, food sliding onto it.

"I left that day. I wanted to live and I didn't want to die here. I didn't want to live with whatever drug you were doing at that point. My baby reframed all of that. And, in a funny way, I don't blame you for not getting it. You didn't know any better. I mean, look at how you were raised—what were you supposed to know about quality of care or diet or hopes and dreams?"

"Careful, little girl," Mrs. Medina growled at Opal.

Opal turned to her. "I don't mean to insult you. But you didn't have many chances either. Your family tucks you out here in this old trailer with a bunch of promises to help you and Davis make a life, then they basically left you alone with about a dollar more than poverty level. That's not fair to you. So, I don't blame you, either, for not protecting me from your son. You didn't know any better," Opal said.

"This better not be about how you think you are so much better than we are," she said, shame stopping her from looking into either Claire's or Opal's eyes.

Opal continued, "No. It's about me. That's what I'm trying to tell you. I've avoided coming back here for these six years—she's six now, Davis, our daughter is—because I was afraid of what you'd do to me."

"He weren't gonna do nothin. You stop that kinda talk," Mrs. Medina said.

"I see that now. But back then, 15 years old? What did I know?" Opal said. "He had me *by the throat*. Did you know that?"

A shocked look. Then a moue of distrust.

"He did. I bet he forgot to tell you that part. Plus, the drugs," Opal said as she turned back to Davis. "I can see those have done you no favors, Davis. Which is why I don't have any fear left. It was Claire's idea to come back and see you. Your daughter wanted to meet you."

Davis hunched uncomfortably in the chair, his glance flashing around the room, unable to settle on any one thing.

Claire tugged on Opal's hand. Looked up at her, silently asking permission to speak. Opal raised an eyebrow, then ticked her head to say yes.

"Mister, if you want, you can come back to our place. We have another house you could stay in. If you want, that is," Claire said.

"What would I do?" he answered.

"Maybe more than you do now, which doesn't seem like much. Dad," Claire tried, "think about it."

She smiled at him, meaning no harm from the assessment.

"I'm not sure my own mama would want me to be that far away," he said doubtfully, looking at his mother.

"Well, you could come with us, too," Opal said to Mrs. Medina. "It's not like you two have much keeping you here, do you? We'd have conditions, but they wouldn't be too tough. If you want, that is."

"Conditions now, from Miss High and Mighty," Davis sneered.

"Everyone's always tryin' to tell us what to do to be better," Mrs. Medina agreed.

Opal and Claire looked at each other, shrugged a shoulder, and turned for the door.

"The offer stands. You'd have to quit the drugs, you'd have to make your own way there, and you'd have to help out with the farm. No stealing. No pay, but you wouldn't have to pay rent, either. Those are pretty good terms. Better than you'd get from most landlords if you ever try to leave this trash heap your family's stuck you in," Opal said. "Here's our phone number. You go on ahead and call if you think you want to give it a try."

"There's a place you can sit and feel better, Mr.—uh, Dad. It's by a spring. I think you'd like it. I'll take you out there if you decide to come visit," Claire said, taking a last full look at the man who fathered her. He sat still, didn't make eye contact.

Claire, realizing her mama was right, followed her out the door—she didn't have a father.

They walked out the door, down the steps. Opal walked to the truck and Claire hunched down to look under the mobile home. She saw the dog curled up, shaking still, and then she got down on her knees.

"Want to come with us, old boy? C'mon, boy. There's all kinds of fun stuff to do."

The dog trembled, and stayed where he was. Opal fired up the old truck, backed out of the yard, and onto the dirt road. She left the gate open and drove away. They weren't sure whether any of the three would ever have the courage to leave. All she knew was that she had tried.

Like Claire asked her to.

Chapter 64

Union County Sheriff missing persons

The sheriff's office in Clayton, New Mexico, was an old, no-nonsense place. It was overfilled with government desks, filing cabinets, and wooden chairs. The front door opened outward, and had done so ever since a huge drunk guy broke the front door down trying to get in to take a poke at the guy the sheriff had in lockup. Although they marveled at the drunk's strength, they also had the carpenter rebuild the door in such a way that entry by forcing the door in was no longer an option. A chest-high counter ran perpendicular to the doorway once a person entered, with waist-high barriers enclosing the entryway into an alcove of sorts. At least the space would slow down a person with ill intent, long enough for an alert deputy to sound an alarm, pull a service weapon, shout a warning. Whatever was needed.

At present, there was a bored male secretary, possibly a deputy, standing at the counter with a landline phone handset cradled between his shoulder and his left ear.

"No, ma'am, we haven't seen an old Saturn around town the past few days," he said with a bored voice.

"No, ma'am, we don't have traffic cameras set up downtown. We don't really have a downtown, though."

He listened for a while, twirled his right finger in a 'move it along' gesture.

"Of course, ma'am. If we do see a tan Saturn driving around, we'll see if we can't catch up to it and ask the drivers to check in with parents. How does that sound?" he asked.

"Of course, ma'am, that's no problem at all. It's all part of the service," he said automatically right before he dropped the phone into the cradle from about a foot above the base.

He wrote in a ledger for a minute or two. He looked up, his eyes stopping on the only other officer in the building. That officer was over in the bullpen, they called it, even though there were just as many female sheriffs as there were male.

"Guess who that was?" he said loudly across the space.

"Your mom?"

"Very funny. It was *a* mom, that's for sure. She'd sent little Billy and Janie out to see her sister in Taos, and they haven't arrived yet. Little Billy and Janie are missing, and could we please go find them? They don't know how to change a tire, Mom says," he sneered.

"Are they really named Billy and Janie?" asked the deputy.

"Naw. They have actual names. But this is pretty much like the annual training scenario those dorks make us do every year."

"Right, that thing is a waste. It always turns out that Billy and Janie are drug addicts and have been just fine. If you call sleeping in their car and stealing for drug money fine."

"You got it. Dale and, uh," he checked his notepad briefly, "Jen haven't shown up in Taos. They were supposed to four days ago. Mom has been working her way west with each little town's law enforcement. Today is our lucky day, I guess," Namith grunted.

"Did you actually commit us to doing any work?" the other deputy, Johnson, asked.

"Nope. I gave her the usual 'if we see anything' line. She was fine with that. She was just checking boxes, I think," said Namith.

Chapter 65

Dale and Jen

Several years after Opal and Claire's sole occupation of Gladstone started, an old Saturn sedan pulled into the Gladstone RV Park and Mercantile. The left front tire of the Saturn had a smashed plastic hubcap, and the nearly bald tire had barely enough air left in it for the driver to navigate the shallow angle of the circle drive. The driver parked the car askew in front of the lone gas pump and turned off the engine. Claire flicked the curtain back in place, and walked back into the kitchen.

"We've got customers, Mom," she said quietly to Opal, who was standing at the kitchen sink washing the four dishes and two spoons from breakfast.

"Here we go again. Whose turn is it to be the greeter?" Opal asked her.

"It's mine. I just wanted to let you know they looked… uh, possible."

"Is that so?"

"Yeah. The car's a piece of junk—it's full of either luggage or trash, it barely runs, and the passenger looks high."

"Ah. Be still my beating heart," Opal said. "Softly now, Claire, let's not scare them away, ok?"

"I'll be as smooth as a breeze through the grass, Mother," Claire assured her. "I can tell they're exhausted. But suspicious, too."

Opal briskly dried the dishes and spoons, dried her hands, and headed out the back door. Claire turned back towards the front, smoothed her hands over her hair, her face, her apron, and walked all the way out to the front porch.

"Hello there," she hollered with a big smile at the doors-still-closed Saturn. "You look like you could use a fresh lemonade and a spell in the shade!"

The window whirred down, getting stuck halfway.

"What'd you say?"

"I said, come on over and sit in the shade for a second. I'll get you some fresh lemonade!"

The window slid back up with a grinding sound, stopping after an inch or two. The two people inside looked at each other, but Claire couldn't tell if they were talking or not. The windshield was smudged and had a film on the inside, like they'd been hotboxing weed more than once on their drive. She assumed it was a male and a female, but couldn't really tell. A decision made, both car doors opened at the same time, and carbon copies stepped out of either side. Long, greasy hair, t-shirts and jeans, flip-flops. The driver's jeans hung off hip bones that jutted forward from a skinny waist and stomach. He, the driver, had a zitty face that he scrubbed the heels of his hands into, pushing upward to push the hair back off his forehead.

The passenger stood wide of the door, leaving it open, and flung her arms wide and back, grunting loudly as she did it.

"Oh, my God, I'm sick of driving. Where the hell *are* we?" she asked over the roof of the car.

"No earthly idea. I just couldn't drive another second so I pulled in here," he said back.

"Looks like our tire is flat, too," said the woman.

Opal had descended the steps by this time—a young, fresh-faced girl, innocent and the opposite of threatening. She continued to smile widely, fixing her gaze on a spot roughly midway between the two.

"You, my friends, have made it to the inimitable Gladstone House. It's true that it's in the middle of nowhere, but we sure do know how to help a carload wash the dust away," Opal said.

"Oh, my God," the girl said again. "That'd be great! Our AC crapped out way back in Kansas."

"It was fine, Jen. It really wasn't that hot," the guy said.

Claire, standing on the porch close to her mother, could tell they'd been having this argument for the last few hours and that they were both sick of it.

"It's nice and cool in the shade up on the porch. Come on, it'll be ok. You don't need to lock the car or anything; you can sit right up there in those rockers and keep an eye on your stuff," Opal said gently.

"I, for one, accept. What you do, Jen, is up to you," he said, starting for the stairs.

"You know good and well that I'm coming up there, too," Jen said. "I have manners, ya know."

She, too, started for the stairs. Claire saw that she actually had Birkenstocks on with mismatched toe socks. The socks, which had slunk down to puddle around her ankles, looked almost muddy, like she'd wandered along the edge of a creek a few days ago and the sludge had almost fully dried. As she passed Claire, who smiled even more brilliantly at her, a foul odor preceded her, then lingered. Organic Chemistry had soundly defeated technology—that girl needed a bath. Claire said nothing about it and didn't let her distaste show on her face. She merely extended each arm to both of the rockers with a table in between.

"Please. Sit. I'll go get two ice-cold drinks. Would you both like lemonade? I have some tea if you'd rather. We even have ice way out here in the middle of nowhere," she laughed.

"Lemonade, please."

"Iced tea, please."

"Coming right up. You just rock a little and lay back. I won't be a second," Claire purred.

She hustled into the kitchen where she quickly filled the tray with glasses full of ice and two small carafes, one each of lemonade and tea.

She noticed, looking out the kitchen window, that her mother had started the grill with some mesquite chunks and had several slabs of meat on a plate right next to it. Opal was scraping the grill while it heated. Waves of heat shimmered above the grate and made her mother's face look melty. Claire turned back to the tray, lifted it, set it back down to add a small loaf of bread and some butter, lifted it again, and headed for the front porch. She nudged the screen door open with her foot and stepped back out.

Chapter 66

Dale and Jen

"We hate to do this to you, little girl," Dale said, "but we are gonna need you and your mom to give us the money you have in that there cash register inside."

He held a shiny revolver in his right hand, and he had it pointed right at her face. He still sat in the rocker, but Jen was not in hers.

"And, please, don't give us any bullshit," Claire heard from behind her. "We're tired and just want to get on our way."

Claire turned her head slightly but stopped quickly when Dale snicked the hammer back on the revolver. She heard feet shuffling, and then the blade of a shovel edged into her peripheral vision, held by Jen.

"Oh, man, you two. Ok, ok…" Claire said placatingly. "Let me just set this down on the table."

She took a step, paused, then looked at Dale for approval. He dipped his chin, a cautious and tiny movement, then flicked his eyes past Claire with a warning glare to Jen.

"No, I get it. No funny business. We—I'm just trying to get you two to relax. I'll just set down the tray. I can't very well go get Mom to get the money if my hands are full, now can I?" she cooed, injecting fear into her voice.

"Fine. But I'll be happy to shoot you. It'll be way easier to get on our way if I did," Dale allowed.

"Just shoot her, Dale," Jen said, exhausted. "I'm sick of her already."

Claire carefully stepped to the table, set the tray down, and turned to face both of them. Dale had tracked her with the revolver and still had it pointed at her face. Claire had begun to sweat, even in the shade of the porch. Her hand shook slightly as she reached for a glass.

Opal came back out on the front porch. She stopped, looked at the visitors, assessed the main plot points, then stepped back and perched on the white rail. The rail was high enough for her to sit comfortably, but still have most of her weight on her feet. She took a deep breath.

"Ok, now look. I know you're tired and exhausted and desperate, which I didn't realize when you pulled up. I bet you're coming down from at least one drug, and your heads are starting to hurt. You're probably on the run, and—"

"I'll thank you to shut the hell up. We don't need any summary of what you think we've been doing for the last few days, and we sure as hell don't need any of your crappy advice, which I'm sure is next," Jen said viciously.

"Oh, no, I wouldn't dream of giving you advice!" Opal said, her hands up disarmingly.

"Good, cuz we shot the last bitch in whatever town that was who tried to get us to see that the Lord would forgive us and all we needed to do was put down our gun and come with her to see her husband, the lawman," Dale growled.

"*No.* Not at *all.* You misread me entirely," Opal urged. "I'll be glad to give you the money. It's somewhere near 724 dollars."

"Bullshit. You'll have thousands somewhere."

"Uh. Look around. This is a fake little RV park in the middle of nowhere, two hours between actual towns that have actual motels and real RV parks. No one stops here. We sell bread, ok?"

"I call bullshit, too," said Jen. She had pulled a folding knife out of her back jeans pocket, and had opened it. The blade was at least four inches long, and it looked deadly sharp. She had set down the shovel once they realized they had the initiative.

"Look! All I'm saying is have a drink, a mouthful of food—you'll feel better. When was the last time you ate?"

Opal asked. "You both look like absolute dog shit."

"Hey! You'd better watch it."

"Or what? You'll shoot me? Knife me? Oh, that's right, you've already threatened all that. Just stop with the drama already. I'm *really* not that scared," Opal said easily.

She sat back on the rail and watched them look at each other to decide. Clearly, she had underestimated their desperation when they pulled up. All the more reason to try.

"It's certainly your choice. Have a drink, eat a bite, then get on your way. Or rush off in your hot car with your stomachs growling, your tire getting flatter, and dehydration setting in," she said carelessly. "You can have the money when you go, either way."

"We *know* it's our choice! We are in charge here. You are just some dumb, ugly blonde working at some stupid fake store who we might just kill for the hell of it. Shut up while we think!" Jen spat at her.

"Go sit at the end of the porch! On the rail!" Dale yelled at her. "You need to be out of reach so we can get a drink."

"You think this is blonde? How sweet—I call it dishwater. But, of course. Happy to do that," Opal replied. "If you can relax, I'll put some steaks on the grill out back. Your call."

She walked slowly backward, watching them the whole time, until she felt the railing of the porch hit her upper hamstrings. She stopped, leaned back on the railing, slowly put her left hand on the corner pillar of the porch. She watched casually, a bored expression on her face, as both Dale and Jen drank straight out of each carafe. Tea and lemonade dribbled past the mouth of the carafe down their grimy faces, onto their shirts. They grabbed for the bread, shoving it hungrily into their mouths.

Chapter 67

Dale and Jen

"So… that's a 'yes' to the steaks?" Opal said with a smile.

Neither of them spoke, their mouths full of bread and drink, but they both nodded. His eyes had closed, and a tear sprang from hers.

Claire glanced at her mother, but said no more. The two starving robbers, distracted by food and drink, didn't notice her leaving. She'd decided to go see what kind of condition Travis's old house was in; she was betting she could talk them into staying there for a few nights. She didn't turn to see if her mother approved of her leaving. She walked across the road to the old shotgun house. It hadn't been lived in since he died, and they rarely went in to see if it was still structurally sound. When she stepped onto the porch, her footprint obvious in the thickened dust, she heard a skittering coming from inside the house. She pulled the screen door open, twisted the cold metal knob of the main door, and walked inside without caution. As she stepped in, a mouse, followed by a second mouse, ran for the far wall and disappeared into seemingly solid wood.

The house smelled worse than musty. It smelled like an old pantry or an old cold storage larder that hadn't been cleaned of perishable food. Had they cleaned it out when Travis finally left them? She couldn't remember. For some reason, the memories surrounding the transition from five of them to just two of them were really quite murky. She remembered being momentarily inconsolable. She remembered that feeling passing quickly, like a summer thundercloud. That pain reshaped much of what she believed about permanence. She had known, from a practical standpoint, that Hazel and Travis would die someday.

A faint memory of Hazel, distraught in the days after her parents' and Nathan's deaths. Claire hadn't lived long enough to brace herself for loss; even though she could pick up some of the feelings from Hazel, and acutely from Shelly, the deaths of Hazel and Travis were her first that she lived entirely and suffered within her spirit. She knew she'd grow, but the first deaths are always the most searing. Because of that, she wanted to help these two hapless souls, needed to help them.

"Hazel would want me to help them," she murmured as she looked around the room.

Since she didn't have any other family—except the failed experiment in finding her birth father—and since Opal was her entire world now, the urge to start with these two kids on the porch blazed clearly, like a Coleman lantern on a pole.

She spent many hours to herself, walking the property, sitting in her room (the front one that used to be storage where Opal and Claire had originally settled), or rocking on any of the porch chairs.

Walking back to the front porch, she found the two still sitting there. They looked less desperate, even if still taut as bowstrings.

"We have a house you could stay in. Just for a few days. Rest up, fix your car," she said. "What do you think?"

Opal looked at Claire with alarm, stepping toward her across the porch.

"Mom, it's ok. We aren't using Travis's house; why shouldn't they?" she said. And to the two, "You could just clean it up a little in exchange."

"Can I talk to you for a second, Claire?" Opal said, this time taking her by the arm and entering the house.

"Excuse us a sec," Claire said with a smile.

They passed into the kitchen, Opal's face darkening to fury, Claire's clearing at the rightness of it.

"Mom, don't you see? This is what Hazel was asking me to do."

"They are trying to *rob* us! They want to take our money and threatened to shoot us, in case you've forgotten all of 20 minutes ago," Opal said.

"That's just their fear and hunger talking. They won't do it. I'm sure of it. Matter of fact, if they are still there when we go back out, I'll be you tomorrow's pig chores that they are gonna stay," Claire said.

"You might be insane, little girl," Opal said. "But I take your bet. I'd love to get out of those messy hogs for once."

Although Jen and Dale didn't stay too long, they both hugged both Opal and Claire in complete trust and friendship when they did. Claire had convinced them to stay long enough to do their laundry, put the spare tire on their old sedan, and eat as much as they could at every meal. They laid themselves down to sleep that first night, and didn't emerge from Travis's house until well after lunchtime the first day. They sat for long spells in the rockers on the porch, dozing off and on. They walked out to the spring and the arroyo. They spent a moment of silence at the memorial rocks that Opal and Claire had placed out there to honor Hazel and Travis. There was no sign of any old adobe house or walls on the road anymore.

In an ironic twist, Opal was almost certain that she had convinced Jen and Dale to make contact with their parents—"You don't want them to worry; just let them know you're ok and pick a time you will call them again," she'd said to them.

Opal was grateful that they didn't ask her if that was what she had done with her own parents.

Chapter 68

Teacher Advertisement

"Claire, you've got to go to school. Or I've got to start homeschooling you," Opal said as they sat on the back porch.

They were weary from a long day of taking care of the farm, like they always did. By the time they finished with the cows and pigs, and had baked for the mercantile, plus ordered supplies to restock the drinks cooler, it was almost always after lunch. And they'd have to start in on the afternoon chores around three or so in order to get done so they could relax after dinner. They'd quit calling it supper after Hazel and Travis died; it seemed like a really old word that no one ever used anymore.

"I don't need school. Why don't you just keep teaching me how to do all this stuff?"

"Well, the state of New Mexico says you have to go to school. It can be here at home, but you can't just grow up and ignore the rules."

"Uh, Mom—we ignore rules all the time, don't we? Who cares if we follow this one?"

"What rules do we ignore?"

"You always drive way faster than the speed limit. That's a rule, right?"

"Yeah, but that's a stupid rule. There's no one to hit if I go faster than what the sign says," she avowed.

"Still. That's a rule. Also, we shoot animals if they are bothering us. Aren't there rules about that?"

"Well. Yes, there are rules about shooting animals. But—those rules are stupid, too!"

"Still a rule."

"If we didn't shoot a coyote now and then, we wouldn't have any calves or any piglets. Those damned coyotes would just get in there and kill everything."

"You shoot raccoons, too. There's a rule not to."

"Raccoons would kill the chickens or stomp all over the eggs if I didn't shoot them! Matter of fact, you maybe better start doing the shooting at raccoons. Make yourself useful around here," Opal laughed.

"Mom! I am useful! I do all the stuff inside here. Cuz you hate it. That's a rule, too, isn't it?" Claire pronounced.

"Hmm… not really a rule, exactly. I just don't want to have to do everything around here so you can be queen for a day."

"I like that game! Queen for a Day—it's my favorite when I get to be the queen," Claire laughed.

They both grinned at each other, a common thread of joy binding them to each other. Opal realized how absolutely lucky she was to have this sweet child right next to her in every step of their lives, and hoped against hope that they could hang on to it as long as possible. Claire smiled, not at her luck, but at the pure, blinding love that shone from her mother when they stayed close and laughed and giggled together.

"Fine. I'll go to school. Where do I have to go?"

"Wait, I just had an idea. What if..." Opal started. "What if we hired a person to work here and be a teacher?"

"You mean to live with us in this house?"

"Well, what if we said they could live over in Travis's house? That would work, wouldn't it?"

"Hey, yeah, that's a good idea! Maybe even a person who has someone I could play with!" Claire shouted.

"Ohh, boy, wouldn't that be cool? Ok, let's get to work on that. We can call this school, too. I can teach you how to advertise. Do you know what that word means?"

"I know the newspaper has advertisers in it. We always throw them away. Or start fires with them."

"Yeah, that's kind of it. But we really need to put a note in the paper or up on a job board that we want to hire someone," Opal said.

"What's a job board?"

"That's a place where you can find a job if you need one, or offer a job if you have one. We can drive into Clayton and put a note up that we are hiring."

"That'd be cool. But can we say we only want to do school half of each day? I do *not* want to learn stuff for an *entire day*!" Claire said stoutly.

"I bet we could say half teacher and half worker. Like we could teach them about the cows and the pigs and the spring and the mercantile on bus days, hmm?"

"You bet, Mom. Should I get the markers and poster paper?"

"Absolutely!"

The poster that Claire ended up making was their third try. It said, in colorful marker, that "a really nice girl needs a teacher to live on the farm and teach her stuff. Also this person could do part-time work taking care of ranch and farm chores. Which the really nice girl can teach her!"

They made several copies of the small poster, all on a bright-white paper with different markers on each copy.

They'd post them when they drove into Clayton next, which was probably going to be this weekend. They tried to drive in on Saturday afternoon, and they could stay for a movie if it was one that they both wanted to see.

Chapter 69

Charlie and Trinidad

They'd gotten a satellite TV dish a few months ago, since it was just the two of them, and they didn't have to argue about whether TV was a waste of time or not. They only got the basic package of channels, but they could still watch the news—and find out they weren't missing anything by not seeing the rest of the world—and the weather to see if they needed to secure the barn tighter.

There were a few channels that always seemed to have shows about fixing your own house up instead of paying someone, and those shows always made the repairs look absurdly easy. It had given Opal several good ideas, though, and she was in the process of putting a stronger pump on the windmill and considering putting a solar panel or two up on the house. There was a ridiculous show about a bunch of workers in an office, and all they did was play dumb jokes on each other and have birthday parties and try to sell paper, but it didn't seem like they worked very hard. Opal and Claire laughed at it, though, and always made popcorn on the stove to eat while they watched it.

Slowly, slowly, they decided they could try to be more of a part of a community. The first step was to see who lived close or who their neighbors were. It was amazing to think that Hazel and Travis had probably known who lived next to them, but that they rarely traveled over to see them or asked them for help, or even offered any help. All those years they had just kept to themselves. It wasn't wrong, exactly. It was just odd. Opal and Claire agreed they would try to change that, and see if they could get to know a larger group of people.

They got some calls about the teaching job. Some odd older people, who—when Opal described the animal chores that went along with the job—quickly said they wouldn't care to do that, and got off the phone. The final call, the person they ended up hiring, turned out to be a young man and his fresh bride from over north of Santa Fe, who were looking to make a new start in a different way. They'd only heard of the job from their own librarian, who had been looking for ways to help this young couple improve their situation.

Their offer was unconventional, in that the young man and his wife offered to teach Claire for nothing, and to help with the chores in exchange for a place to stay and sharing in the house duties. Opal invited them to come visit, and they said they would. They picked a date less than a week away, and at the agreed-upon day and time, an old Ford F-150 clattered into the circle drive in front of the house. A young man, white but tanned by outside work, stepped out and a woman, darker with either Latina or Native blood, stepped down from the passenger's seat. They both smiled from under their cowboy hats, and joined hands as they walked towards the front steps up to the wide porch of Gladstone.

"Good afternoon. I'm Charlie, and this is Trinidad," he said smoothly.

"A pleasure to finally meet you, Charlie. And hello to you, Trinidad," Opal said with a smile.

"I love your matching hats!" Claire said.

"I bet you are Claire. Am I right?" Trinidad said with a grin.

"Yep. I'm the student. And you guys are the teachers."

"Please, sit down. I have tea."

They sat, arranged on the porch on one of the many fine afternoons one can find in the Southwest, as long as there is a bit of shade and a sip of something to quench one's thirst.

After a few moments of quiet, Charlie said, "So. Here's my idea. I haven't had a ton of school myself. But Trinidad here is smart as a whip. I was thinking, hoping, that maybe we could do a modified home-school system where we all kind of help each other learn whatever we are best and worst at. I don't think I could stand to go to any more classes in a community college or a high school or any program where I'd have to put up with people who are idiots. I just don't have the patience," he admitted.

"I've finished high school and one year of community college. So I don't technically have a college degree, and of course I'm not a 'certified' teacher," Trinidad said, twitching her fingers around the word, "but, like Charlie said, I'm pretty smart, and I think we could figure out what Claire is good at and what she needs help with, and we could all work on it together."

"And, before you say no, we want to say that this wouldn't be permanent and, if it doesn't work out, you won't have any trouble getting us back out of the house you said would come along with the job. I'm saying give us a year, or maybe six months, and we can see how we all feel about it," Charlie said.

"Yes, Mom! Let's do it! I like them," Claire shouted.

Opal put her hand on Claire's shoulder, patting her gently while she smiled.

"I do think the idea has promise," Opal allowed. "I'm curious, though, why you said on the phone you needed a change of scenery for a while?"

Charlie and Trinidad looked at each other, soberly at first, then cracked up with laughter.

"That right there, Miss Opal and Miss Claire, is a long story. I bet we could tell you and be done by sunrise," Charlie said with a chuckle.

"It's nothing bad, though. It all ended well. We just needed to let our small village calm down a little before we go back and stir things up again," Trinidad said, smiling at Claire.

"Well, let's try it, I guess," Opal declared, reaching one hand to each of them to shake on it.

Epilogue

Thus ends the tale of Gladstone—at least this chapter. It remains to be seen if the teaching arrangement works out to mutual satisfaction. It remains to be seen if Opal and Claire decide to stay at Gladstone, or decide they want to move away. There is a possibility that they will want to trail Charlie and Trinidad back to live in that village, which is full of love and support, and always has room for another set of underdogs.

Acknowledgements

Though writing can be a solitary business, I am very grateful for the help and support I've received along the way from a great many people and organizations. Thank you to SCBWI (Society of Book Writers and Illustrators) which has chapters all over the world and was the first place I sought inspiration and guidance. The Kansas/Missouri Chapter of SCBWI hosts a Writing Retreat at a monastery in Missouri where I spent several weekends working on my craft of writing. Way-Word Writers, started by my friends and colleagues Heather, Stephanie, and Nicki, hosted a Writing Retreat in Branson that was trajectory-changing for my writing and for this book, in particular. I will always remember the evenings where we read our work to each other for the sheer joy of hearing the creativity of writers. Kansas Writers Association is a very supportive group that meets monthly in Wichita; thanks for all of your positivity and expertise. Harvester Arts in Wichita, KS, invited me to their 2024 Artist INC cohort; I'll be forever grateful for the opportunity they gave me. They work hand in hand with Mid-America Arts Alliance supporting artists at all stages of creativity in a six-state area. David Wayne Reed, of M-AAA, said career-changing things to me in our Artist INC post-cohort collaboration meeting. Laura, from Plot Twist Edit, gave me meaningful feedback for Gladstone. My thanks to Dominick Wakeford, my editor found through Reedsy – you've helped me shepherd this book across the finish line. The beautiful cover art is by my friend and colleague Taoimah Rutledge. Thanks to LC Photography for the headshot session. To the dozens of people who I've bounced ideas off of for the past few years... thank you for listening. I say a million thanks to all those organizations, and to the passionate creatives that run them, for your support and encouragement.

Angie, none of this makes sense without you in my life. Thanks for your always-present support and cheerleading and belief and love.

Be on the lookout for Charlie and Trinidad's story—there's a lot to tell you—and get ready to read about Claire growing into her full stewardship of Gladstone.